where
DEMONS
hide

A.M. BROOKS

Where Demons Hide
By A.M. Brooks
Copyright © 2019 A.M. Brooks

Note: This story may not be suitable for persons under the age of 18.
Cover and Formatting: Cassy- Pink Ink Designs
Editing: Ellie- My Brother's Editor
Proof Reading: Athena and Darlene- Lit Up PR

Acknowledgments

My Husband- Thank you for stepping up to care for our littles when I need time in the cave. For never making me feel bad about chasing this dream. For being the best human possible and saying the right things when I'm freaking out.

My Family- Thank you for continuing to be supportive and cheering me on. I love running my ideas past you. Special shout out to my brother….our relationship and your personality really drove me to create the best dynamic in this book. It was emotional inspiration.

Kiki and Colleen- The Next Step PR -Thank you for your hard work, dedication, and guidance. Book three and I would still be lost without your check-ins, lists, calendars and reminders. I'm getting there, I promise!

Ellie- My Brother's Editor- ….I'm so sorry that you have to deal with my grammar and messy draft versions. Thank you for making my words beautiful.

Cassy - Pink Ink Designs- For taking the time to pull together my vision, then the second vision, and working with me thru it all. The cover is hot!

My Beta readers- Thank you for your positivity and willingness to critique if needed. Again, I appreciate your time and putting yourselves out there with ideas, teasers, and changes. The extra pairs of eyes is so helpful!

My Readers- Thank you for your purchase. It is because of you that I can continue to write and live my dream. I hope you enjoy Blaise and Jay's story as much as I did while writing it.

Blake's Playlist

The Sound of Silence- Disturbed
Smells Like Teen Spirit- Nirvana
Scar Tissue- Red Hot Chili Peppers
All Apologies- Nirvana
Blurry- Puddle of Mud
The Unforgiven- Metallica
Sex on Fire- Kings of Leon
Chop Suey!- System Of A Down
Kryptonite- 3 Doors Down
Rollin' (Air Raid Vehicle)- Limp Bizkit
The Pretender- Foo Fighters
Bodies- Drowning Pool
Down with the Sickness- Disturbed
Are you Ready- Disturbed
Bawitdaba- Kid Rock
Debonair- Dope
Broken- Seether feat. Amy Lee
Only God Knows Why- Kid Rock
Comedown- Bush
Cowboy- Kid Rock
Hemorrhage (In My Hands)- Fuel
She Talks to Angels- The Black Crowes
Cocky- Kid Rock
Let Me Live/Let Me Die- Des Rocs
Never Too late- Three Days Grace
Devil Without a Cause- Kid Rock
Best of You- Foo Fighters
Coming apart- Red
Headstrong- Trapt
I Hate Everything About You- Three Days Grace
Far Behind- Candlebox
Secret Garden- Bruce Springsteen
Butterfly- Crazy Town
Hanging By A Moment- Lifehouse
Shine- Collective Soul
When I'm Gone- 3 Doors Down
Click Click Boom- Saliva
Hear You Me- Jimmy Eat World
Ain't No Rest for the Wicked- Cage The Elephant
The World I know- Collective Soul
In The Shadow Of The Valley Of Death- Marilyn Manson
Angels Fall – Breaking Benjamin
Lost Boy- Ruth B.
Demons- Imagine Dragons
Spotify Playlist:

https://open.spotify.com/user/ashtonbm8/

playlist/5gf7WjWzaJPIXuo4D5D40f?si=zH822TyWSlq_qMevYVkR1A

Dedication

Brothers and Sisters.
The brothers who annoy their sisters.
The sisters who mother their brothers.
The brothers who protect.
The sisters who shelter.
The brothers who know her secrets.
The sisters who hold his hands during hard times.
The grief, the feuds, the secrets, the joys, and the love that holds us
together no matter the distance we live or the age we grow old to.
It's a relationship like no other.

where
DEMONS
hide

What happens in Vegas...

A.M.B

Prologue

DON'T USUALLY DO THIS. I HAVE NEVER felt this out of control or this in tune with another person before. Correction, a stranger before. I'm not the girl that has one-night stands. Hell, I've only had sex with one person and that was when I lost my virginity in my junior year of high school. This just isn't me. When I walked into this rundown, hole-in-the-wall dive bar three hours ago, underage, mind you. This was not how I pictured things going. My fake ID got me the drinks I needed and the buzz I chased. The wannabe fraternity boys at the pool table were the distraction I wanted. I don't know what it is, but something about a girl without a shine in her eyes and a bitch attitude drives boys wild. They want what they think they can't have. And they definitely couldn't have me.

When *he* walked in, the energy in the goddamn room changed. The tiny hairs on my arms stood up. A burn of awareness slid down my spine, sending warmth flowing through my muscles. It was the warmest I'd been all day after standing in the rain for hours. He had my attention when his huge body pressed against mine as I leaned against the bar like I owned the place. Whether he could sense the storm inside me or feel the numbness rolling off my skin, I'll never know. I was drawn to him, and he was pulling me along for the ride.

"Come with me." Three words spoken in a deep east coast accent and I was shaken. A command that spoke to my soul and I would follow wherever. Including down the dark hallway and right inside the women's restroom.

No talking, no foreplay, just a rip of a condom wrapper before he grips my ass and hauls me up against his body, pinning me to the wall with his hips. I welcomed the ache, the burn, the sensation of being too full that it's almost painful. My black dress is bunched around my hips. His eyes, the deepest brown I had ever seen with eyelashes any girl would envy, search mine. Asking too many things and reading too many secrets. His mouth swoops down, molding his lips on mine, possessive and dangerous. His tongue pries my lips apart to tangle with my own. Fucking my mouth like it wasn't the first time I'd ever tasted him. I was definitely doing this. My arms held around his shoulders tighter with each deep thrust of his body into mine. I could feel every impact of my shoulder blades colliding with the hard wall and I didn't care. I would probably have scratch marks there afterward and I gave zero fucks. It was dirty and raw. All that mattered to me was the way his fingers gripped my waist, pushing me higher up the wall before he used his mouth to pull the collar of my dress down. Sharp teeth clamped down on my lace covered nipple causing me to cry out.

"Let go," his voice whispered against my lips as he drew back to look at me. Our eyes colliding at the same time as he pushes me over the edge. I feel my body fall apart and melt against that wall.

My heart cracks open, letting tidal waves of emotion spring free. My orgasm runs through me, making my legs shake and toes curl. I had no words for how he made me feel.

It was the first time I'd felt anything all day... the first time I'd experienced any emotion in the weeks since the accident. This stranger gave me more than a mind-blowing orgasm. He gave me a way to forget I'd just buried the only family I had... my brother.

One

PEOPLE SAY THE LONELIEST NUMBER IS one. When you have been part of a two your whole life, that statement is cold and desolate. I was alone. A one. I had to be strong on my own and fight by myself. After *that* night, the night of the funeral, I went home, balled myself up in the bottom of the shower and released all the pain that had been eating my insides for over a week. I was no longer numb. That was three months ago. I fought all summer long to bottle down the loneliness. I knew I had to keep living. Blake would have wanted that for me.

With the summer almost over, I had finally got to the point where I can hold a conversation if absolutely needed, my lips would crack into a smile. What I could not stand was one more person asking me how I was doing. I was going to punch someone in the face if that continued. I worked full time at Señor Loco to fill the void and to help make rent. It also forced me to be social and find my new normal. Something I really hated and attempted to avoid at all costs. No matter how nice I could be, there was always someone who didn't seem to know how to filter their thoughts from their brain to their mouth. *Seriously! Did this chick just ask me if she could look through Blake's things for her shirt?*

"Your shirt is not there. I promise." Was all I could grit out to her stupid fake blonde bimbo face. Kinley Adams had been the Queen Bitch at the high school back in the day. Head cheerleader, student council, you name it, she was probably the head of it. She was beautiful in the made-up, plastic-looking way. Her family had also been from money and bought her everything she wanted. The only thing she had not been able to obtain had been respect from my brother or his group of friends.

"Well, is there any way it could have been misplaced? I know I left it there, and this was like back before senior prom. It's from the Nickelback concert." Her voice whined while she sat sipping her strawberry daiquiri through a straw.

"Again, I assure you it was not in his room." I take a deep breath and start counting in my head *three, two, one…*

"Like oh my god, Blaise, can you just look again? It was a really big deal to him to buy me that shi—"

"Are you fucking kidding me?" I spit out, slamming down the glass mug I had been holding, sloshing beer all over my hand. "Blake hated Nickelback. He never would have bought you tickets, let alone stood in line to buy their damn t-shirt! I cleaned his room myself. No t-shirt. Besides, fucking whores from Chaparral was not really his thing." I was breathing heavily now. I knew my face was red, tears pricked the edges of my eyes. My fist tightens around the glass as I was imagining it to be her skinny, pale neck.

"Palmer, take five, will ya," Luis shot at me stepping out from his side office. He must have finally realized where this whole conversation was going. Kinley on a stretcher.

"Yeah, whatever," I muttered as I push my way past him out the back through the side door. I needed air. I needed to get out of this bar. Too bad I still had six hours left to go in my shift. This day was getting worse by the minute. I wrapped my arms around myself, feeling chilled despite the desert heat. I was tired of people wanting to ask for Blake's stuff or if Blake had any of their stuff. Some of these pretenders didn't even know him except for occasionally running into him at a party or at The Scar.

Gathering my long black hair off my neck, I paced around the back parking lot, breathing deeply and letting the tension roll off me. Nothing has been the same. I was left all alone. The guys started flaking off. True, I didn't answer their phone calls, but I was pissed. We were supposed to be a family. When one of your own dies, you stick around a lot longer than till after the funeral. Except if you're Seth, because he didn't even bother to show up at all. I get it, Seth and Blake were tight, but so were Blake and I. We shared more than the same DNA. Even though we were three years apart in age, Blake had raised me when the woman we call mom couldn't. Our sperm donor hadn't stuck around long enough for me to know him or for Blake to even know how to say the word dad. I hadn't even bothered to find him to let him know about the funeral. It had always been just Blake and me. Now it was just me. I had no idea what I was doing half the time. I felt like I was sinking. It was time to decide what I wanted to do for the rest of my life and I was avoiding it.

"Palmer, I said five minutes, not a lunch break," Luis yelled out the door. "You have company, don't take long. April just sat you a three top by the bar."

"Yes, sir." I saluted to him as I whisked back inside.

I generally like Luis for the most part. He was gruff at forty-five and looked like he had the body of a teddy bear. I didn't like to piss him off. He gave me a job when I wanted to help Blake make our rent so we could stay in Nevada. In the past, Luis had often turned his head the other way if I stole a can of tomatoes and didn't ask questions when we would take off to Las Vegas once a month. During that time, Blake and the guys would work at the hotels as any type of help that was needed. Many times I went with, even when I got to the age where I could stay behind if I had wanted. The guys never made me feel awkward about being the little sister. I had been adopted by all of them. Too bad that courtesy didn't last past identifying Blake's body at the morgue.

Sergeant Ramirez was waiting for me at the bar when I got back inside. Normally a uniformed cop in a bar would make visitors nervous, but locals never had a problem with it. I shook my head. Even Ramirez had managed to check on me more than the guys had in the past three months. At first, it had been every day, which was annoying. Now his visits were weekly, and I looked forward to seeing him. Mostly I just liked to push his buttons. Some habits never die.

"What's hot today, Sarge?" I asked him in my overly sweet waitress voice.

"Seriously?" he asked, rolling his eyes at my question. It was obvious he noted the sarcasm in my voice. I tipped my head to the side, watching him, not apologizing and just waiting for him to continue.

"I received a call from Seth this morning." His eyes narrowed slightly as he looked at me. "I was wondering if he contacted you like he said he was going to."

"I haven't heard from the kid in months, Sarge," I say, shrugging my shoulders. "I don't even know if I could talk to him without reaching through the phone to strangle him." The other guys pulling away irritated me but I could handle it. Not Seth, though. He was different. He had been my best friend, too. My first kiss, my first love, my first everything, and he bailed.

Sarge looked down at the counter, his brow furrowed in thought, not even batting an eye at my empty death threats. "Something sounded off with him," he said worriedly. "That's why I'm asking. I'm sure it's nothing. He just sounded... flat." His warm gaze lifted back to me.

I look away. "Well, apparently he is very devastated by what happened to Blake." Again the sarcasm leaked into my voice. Sarge looked at me a little softer now. He knew how I felt about the guys all ditching out after the funeral. "Look, not to be rude, but I have a table and it's almost the lunch rush, so..."

"Yeah, I'm heading out," he said, raising his hands in surrender. "One more thing, Pricilla wants you to stop by for dinner tomorrow evening. She said she would make your favorite. Plus, Katy and Nico are wanting to see you again."

"Sure," I replied even though I did not want to be social. I went out of my way to avoid people as much as I could. Pricilla was hard to say no to. Plus, if I didn't go, it'd be just another night eating a PB&J at home by myself.

"Bueno, I'll let her know. If you hear from Seth, try and see where he is. Like I said, he sounded... different." Worry was etched in the deep lines on his face.

"Got it." I waved him off.

"Adios," he answered before slipping out the door, back into the bright Nevada sun. One look at the clock let me know I still had five long hours to go in my shift. I didn't want to be worried about Seth. He made his bed and now he had to lie in it. Instead, I pasted on a smile and embraced the sugary waitress voice, as I headed to my new tables.

I imagined Blake sitting at the far corner of the bar next to the pool tables like he always did. He would be smiling if he was here, probably chatting up one of the regulars or a pretty girl from out of town. I'd put in an order of mozzarella sticks for him because he was always hungry and I wouldn't want him to fill up on just beer. He had to be sober enough to drive me home. Luis would come out and give him a hard time about being a permanent fixture and if he wanted a job here, too. I can still hear Blake's laugh, the rumble that comes from deep in the chest. Heartfelt and real. Other people would smile just because he sounded like he was having a good time. And, he would really laugh at Luis' suggestion. He'd make it up later though by inviting his never-ending parade of friends to join him creating more business for Señor Locos. Blake never ran out of friends. He was naturally someone people were drawn to; someone people could trust. He worked hard at any odd job he could. He even had time to fit in a few credits at the community college. Something I hadn't known about until after his death. Guilt had plagued me for days. My brother had been running all over the place working, going to school, and taking care of me. It hit me hard that it probably had been too much on him. That he most likely was exhausted, stretched thin; that his body had given up, and that tree had been collateral damage.

My fingers curl around the edge of the tray I'm carrying. My lungs fight to work because, for a second, just a small amount of time when I look at that corner, I can still picture him there. Still being my hero. Watching and smiling.

Two

Buzz...BUZZ...*buzz...buzz...*

"What the...?" My head shoots off my pillow, squinting at the clock by my bed, the red numbers read *two* a.m! Who was calling me? Fear and anxiety raced through my body; the last time I got a call this early—

"Hello," I answered the phone feeling my stomach turning and cold sweat started to break out over my brow.

"Hey Blaisy, sorry if I woke you up." Relief, then anger flash through my mind.

"What do you want, Antonio?" I bit back. Yeah, I was hanging by a thread.

"I deserve that. I'm sorry I haven't been around much since... since Blake died," he says. His voice laced with guilt.

"No, you haven't. You all left. You all left me." I could hear my voice getting louder. My body shuddering with rage. I was ready to explode or cry. All I could hear was silence on the other end of the line.

"Blaise." His voice cracks. "You're right, I did leave and you have every right to be mad. I'm sorry. It was just weird being there, ya know? Everywhere I went, I was like, 'oh this is where Palmer and I went Fridays before the game.' It was just hard, ya know?" he says, sounding like the broken boy he was when we first met.

I bite my bottom lip to stop from crying. I never thought I'd hear that much emotion from Antonio. He usually was the laid back one in the group who just rolled with the punches. I only ever heard him get really worked up if it was about a hot chick or a bad game of Call of Duty. Maybe I never thought about how these guys felt losing Blake either.

"Yeah, I know," I whisper. "So, are you guys in Vegas then?"

"Yup. That's actually why I'm calling. Well, two reasons actually. Stone, Joey, and I will be back this week. Summer break is over and we raked in some cash." He sounds pleased with himself.

"Just you, Stone, and Joey?" I questioned. What the fuck about Seth?

"Yeah, that's the other reason I was calling. Stone was wondering if you've heard from Seth at all?" The uneasiness in his voice raises goosebumps up my arms and across the back of my neck.

"Why does everyone keep assuming I've heard from Seth? I haven't heard from him in over six months. He didn't make it to the funeral, in case you don't remember." I was getting pissed. "I thought he was with you guys."

Again there was silence.

"Toni."

"Yeah, sorry, um, no, he didn't meet up with us. What do you mean everyone keeps assuming you've seen him?"

"Sergeant Ramirez just asked me the same thing today. He said Seth called him and apparently he may be contacting me," I tell him, totally confused with the situation. What was going on?

"Oh, cool... well, I'll let ya get back to sleep, Blaisy. See you later this week then?" He pauses, waiting for me. A small part of my heart leaps to life knowing they will be in town soon.

"Yup, see ya," I answer before hitting the end button and setting my phone back down. I lay back against my pillow and listen to the silence in the apartment. Any minute now she'll come home, hang her keys, pour a drink, and then I'll hear her bedroom door close. More silence. We had this routine down perfectly. I lived around her and she existed around me.

Anger burned my chest. Parents were allowed time to be depressed when they lose a child. They deserve a chance to grieve and to mourn. It's unnatural for a parent to lose a child while they are still alive. Our mom had been absent for so long, she didn't deserve to act like she was grieving. She didn't deserve to wallow in her own self-pity. If anything, she was to blame. Blake worked his ass off to help provide for us. Any money she made came and went as fast as the bottles in her liquor cabinet. I didn't feel sorry for her. I didn't feel sad for her. That was the real problem though... she was my mom, and I felt nothing for her.

I decided right then I was definitely going to dinner at the Ramirez's house tonight. Anything to be away from the silence seemed like a better choice. I more or less lived alone the way it was; the way it had been for years. She was home when she was in town. Being a stewardess kept her away a lot and Blake and I had never minded. Our lives had functioned just fine without her.

I moved back in after the funeral to help her and because I could no longer afford the apartment Blake and I had subleased when he turned eighteen. We had gone up in scale and could afford it with both our jobs and occasional rent from whoever was crashing for a couple of days. On my own, I had to let the lease go. It about killed me to do it. I remembered the day Blake picked me up from school and drove me there. I thought he was kidding when he said he signed a lease. I thought I had died when he asked if I wanted to live with him instead of our mom.

I'd give anything to be back in that bedroom listening to the sounds of Call of Duty echoing from the living room because the silence… the silence is too much.

Three a.m. now… I roll over,
hear the lock click,
pull the covers up to my chin,
she kicks off her shoes,
I close my eyes,
hear the clink of ice hitting her glass,
I concentrate on breathing,
hear as she walks down the hallway and her door closes.
I fall back asleep.

THE NEXT AFTERNOON at four p.m., my shift ends. Another day of emptying ketchup bottles, dealing with heckling children, and dirty men asking for my number passed by quickly. I never heard from Antonio or the others, so I assume they will just arrive one day out of the blue. And, again, Seth never called. I was starting to feel like a dejected girlfriend for how often I was looking at my phone and I hated it.

I punch out on my time card and tip the busboys generously. On the way to the Ramirez's, I grab a bouquet of daisies, which I know

Pricilla will like. It has been awhile since I visited. My stomach grumbled, clueing me in to the idea that I had made a good choice in accepting the dinner invite.

The Ramirezs lived out of town on a private road. As I drove toward their property, I could see the horses running around their pen while a few grazed farther away. Katy and Nico were leaning on the fence when I pulled up but were soon launching themselves at my car.

"Blaise, come see my new horsey." Katy animatedly ushers me over to the pen. At ten years old, she was the spitting image of her mom. Her black hair is parted in pigtails, her shorts are dusty, and she has a few pieces of straw stuck to the fabric of her purple tank top. Once he sees me, Nico pretends to ignore me, as he normally does unless boy things were being discussed. He's eight going on eighteen; broody and wild.

"Isn't she pretty?" Katy asks, grabbing my hand and pulling me closer to her new amber brown and white American Paint Horse. "I named her Aurora after the princess," Katie explains.

"Very nice," I tell her. "It suits her well."

"Do you have a new horse too, Nico?" I ask while ruffling his hair.

"Eww! You're messing up my flow," he rants back while frantically trying to push his heavy dark locks back in place. Katy shakes her head and I laugh at his attempts. Pricilla will have her hands full with him someday.

"Hola, Blaise! Niños, it's time to eat!" Pricilla ushers us all inside and I hand her the small bouquet before finding my seat.

"Gracias, you did not have to," she continues to talk as she cut the ends. She places the bouquet in a vase, setting it on the dinner table before pulling me into a hug.

"I just wanted to thank you for having me for dinner." I smile, pulling back to look at her. Pricilla is infectious that way. Even in the worst days after the accident, Pricilla was the only one who could get me to smile and forget just for a few moments. She is also the only reason we didn't starve. Most of the community stopped by to pay their respects, but Pricilla brought food every day, rain or shine.

"Where is Sarge?"

"He took a call in his office, he'll be out shortly. We can start; let's say grace," she announces, grabbing our hands. Same as always, I bowed my head and joined only at the Amen.

Dinner is amazing and fills that empty hole in my stomach. Pricilla's spaghetti was my favorite and I could tell that the marinara was made from scratch. It easily brought back the tough-on-your-stomach and tight-in-your-chest memories. The boys and I had been frequent dinner guests at the Ramirez home growing up. Long before Katy and Nico were born. Long before Pricilla had her first horses to care for and Sarge was still just a patrol officer.

"Sorry about that," Sarge says as he slides into his chair at the end of the table. He had been absent for almost the whole meal.

"Is everything alright, Tomas?" Pricilla asks as she hands him a Corona from the fridge.

"Si, it will be. Everyone tell me about your day," he replies, his eyes moving over everyone and avoiding me.

Katy and Nico excitedly tell their dad about what the new horses were doing and how their neighbor Joel fell off the tube in the deep end at the community pool. Katy entertains us by re-enacting the whole story about how she had to help pull him to the shallow area because he couldn't swim well; poor Joel.

Pricilla goes next and tells us that the camp went well today. That this was the last week before the kids went back to school.

Pricilla's horse camp was how Blake and I had met and became friends with Seth and Joey. The horses and horseback riding were used for therapy. Blake and I had been sent to camp after a couple behavioral disturbances at school. Mostly, other kids trying to pick on Blake and for him fighting back with his hands. Then of course, I intervened to protect my big brother, not that I could do much because they were always older and bigger than me. By the fifth time, the school called social services who paid a visit to our mom. In order to do the minimum requirements, she sent us to therapy for behavior management as suggested to Pricilla's camp.

On our first day at camp, we met Seth Baird. He was a little anxious, brown-haired boy who was sent to live with his grandma after his father was arrested. PTSD was his diagnosis, but he was mostly just quiet. He was just two years older than me, but also stuck to Blake like I was. We were inseparable.

The following summer, Joseph Williams became a member of camp Caballo Blanco. He was also a fighter and after some toeing the alpha line, he and Blake finally became friends. We were the fabulous four and inseparable. Each of us had a rough start and each of us had a guiding hand from Pricilla. We were fed and had a place to nap securely if needed. A person to talk to when going home felt like an unsafe option.

Stone and Antonio Garcia are cousins and showed up at our school when I was in the eigth grade. Blake and Antonio had classes together in the tenth grade with Seth. Stone and Joey began ruling the upperclassmen in the eleventh grade. They walked a line between people fearing them or just in awe of them. I was grandfathered in because I was Blake's sister, but they made me feel included. I was considered a special prize by the time I hit ninth grade and we all went to the same high school. I learned fast that the girls either wanted to be my friend to get to the guys or they hated me. *Slut* was my nickname for the first two days of high school. Immature and so wrong of them to assume that calling me names would gain them an in with the guys either. Boys aren't catty like girls. They tell you how it is, and they didn't care if the girl's feelings got hurt. The girls learned really quick after that, calling me names got them exiled or hurt, like the time I punched Susie Anderson. After that, I became closer with Sarge.

"And what about you, Blaise, how was your day?" he asks me while still avoiding looking at me.

All four pairs of eyes swing to me. "It was fine. I worked, then got to hang out with you all." I shrugged my shoulders. It felt normal to talk with people about my day. I was once again reminded of the silence waiting for me back at the duplex. Suddenly, the food felt too heavy in my stomach.

"If you're done, you should walk with me. There is something I want to talk more about with you," Sarge said. He was already standing up and moving away from the table.

"Uh, sure." I scrambled to follow him out onto the front steps. We started walking toward the horse pen. From inside the house, I can hear Nico and Katie running upstairs to watch television before bed, and Pricilla clearing the dishes.

By now, the sun had cleared the horizon. The sky was filled with stars, which were easier to see out here away from the city lights. The slight breeze played with my long hair. I remember Blake telling me, after we lost our dog, that all the stars were people and animals in heaven that we love. A quick look up to the sky causes my breath to catch, and my gaze to become watery. I want to imagine my brother as every star so that he is everywhere. I don't want to be alone.

"It's about Blake, Blaise," Sarge says suddenly, his voice gruff and hesitant. As if what he is about to say has been weighing on him. My eyes immediately snap to his face. For the first time I notice how preoccupied he looks. I can see the purple smudges under his eyes, a look of concern staring back at me. I don't say anything and wait for him to continue.

"Look, there is some information that is being looked at about the crash. We had our ends tied up here, but there are some higher-ups in Vegas that want the case still open," he says, watching me, waiting for my reaction.

I keep my face masked and wiped of emotion. I can't form a sentence anyway. *Blake's case is still open.* The words cause my chest to tighten and my heart pumps so hard and fast I can feel my pulse trying to jump out of my body.

"I don't understand," I finally say, my tongue darting out to lick my lips. This information doesn't make sense. "He flipped his car driving too fast like he always did. Like I always asked him not to," I explain to Sarge, my brain still trying to process. "He didn't have control. He wasn't invincible. He wasn't made of steel. How can any of that need to stay open for some higher up asshat to look at?"

"I don't know, Blaise." Sarge looks down at the ground, his large hand resting on the back of his neck. I instantly felt bad about my outburst yet Sarge didn't seem as stunned as I thought he would be. He expected I'd act like this. I knew I sounded angry. I was angry at my dead brother. Angry that he left me for a few thrills of driving over the speed limit.

"So what does this mean? He's buried, we had a funeral. He died six months ago."

"I know. I'm sorry to have to be telling you this right now," he replies, running his hands over his buzz cut. "Apparently they are sending someone down here to talk with you more about this. That's who I was on the phone with this evening. I'm supposed to tell you to listen for the Irish," he says, slinging his arms over the top of the fence.

I pause. "What the fuck! Is this a joke? My brother dies and his case is remaining open so the Irish can talk to me." I can hear my voice getting louder and I can't seem to control it. I see Sarge's eyes dart to the screen door where Pricilla is watching us. My hands shake, my chest tightens, and my knees want to give way. I can't breathe and every thought is painful. *What was happening?* Nothing has been normal, but at least my life was settling into a routine again. I could feel the cold start to work its way back in, blackness was edging around my vision.

"I'm sorry, Blaise," Sarge says, pulling me into his side and holding me together. The panic inside threatens to claw its way out. Sarge rubs my arm soothingly. "This is out of my jurisdiction for now," he whispers. "We're here though. When you know more and need to talk, you can always come here, okay?"

Fuck this. My life has been turned upside down. Friends have bailed for the summer or for college, and my mom is a living nightmare lost in her own problems.

"Yeah, okay," I say, yanking myself from his embrace and walking fast to my car. I rub my hands up and down my jeans for warmth. I get in and slam down on the accelerator, sending a cloud of dust into the air behind me.

Sarge watches my car leave the driveway. Another quick glance in my rearview mirror, I can see Pricilla watching from the front porch. It's not until I'm a few yards down the road that I crank Limp Bizkit's "Rollin'" as I roll my window down and suck in huge gulps of fresh air. Everyone has lost their damn minds. The cold was back, settling into my chest and squeezing around my heart again. Fuck, Blake.

I sped home, grateful that I don't meet another car until I turned into the parking lot. I say a quick thanks to the cosmos that my mom will not be here tonight. She has to jet set back to the Midwest. I would be alone and all I wanted was to escape. I needed to run. I grabbed my old sneakers and some earbuds before I take off.

I push my muscles to exhaustion in order to feel the pain in my ribs as I breathe harder. *Is someone getting the best, the best, the best, the best of you* blared through my ears until I can't hear the thoughts in my head; only the pounding of the rock music and my own breathing. I need it this way. No noise, just the miles under my feet as I push harder. Each slap of my feet against the pavement sending vibrations up my legs. It had been months since I last ran. It felt like forever since I was a senior, in my blissed-out mind thinking about graduating and spending the summer with my brothers in Vegas. Track was my passion that Blake also enjoyed. As soon as Mom left on Sunday mornings, we were running around town, pushing each other to beat our previous times. God, I fucking missed those days.

By the time I got back, my knees were weak, and I shuddered from the mixture of my damp clothes and the slight arid breeze. It was one a.m. *Nothing good happens after midnight*, Blake used to say. I fell on my bed, just listening to the silence and the fan turning above me. I wanted to leave. I wasn't supposed to be back here of all places. Vegas then college, that was what we had been talking about, planning for. We didn't have a lot of money, but Blake promised we could cover it.

"I have it taken care of, Blaise. Trust me," he said, pulling on the ends of my braided hair. I did trust him. I let my hopes get high and my dreams big.

The little savings I did have stashed away I ended up using to pay for the funeral. After Blake died, I lost all desire to continue our plan. It wasn't the same, and I was scared to do it without him. I had no one backing me in my corner and I felt trapped in the life I had created over the past five months. Honestly, I didn't even think I could leave the place where I grew up with my brother. That was the sad, pathetic truth. I slam my eyes closed against the single tear that leaks down my cheek.

"What do I do?" I whisper into the darkness. I imagine he would study my face, taking in all my emotions. He would saunter over to the bed and lay down next to me. Kiss my head and say, *We'll do it together. It's taken care of. We don't give up.*

Three

"ARE YOU GOING TO PICK UP THAT ORDER or just watch the fries burn?" Luis asks as he pushes the food order toward me.

"Sorry," I mumble and hoist the tray over my shoulder.

Luis' normal stern face softens a bit as I turn to go. The night was busy at Señor Loco. The door revolving since I started my shift at five. I sailed by barely noticing anyone around me. Pretty sure the last table stiffed me on my tip due to my less than warm demeanor. In my defense, my mind was preoccupied thinking about the conversation with Sarge the other night after dinner. It had been a few days since, and I was losing my mind. I constantly felt on edge and was overthinking everything people said to me waiting for this Irish prophet.

I was driving myself crazy and I knew I probably was on Luis' last nerve, too. He kept me busy tonight behind the bar and running food during downtimes. I was grateful to him for that.

"Two more Dos Equis please, Blaise," Jenna says, loud enough to clear my haze.

"Coming," I answer, grabbing the bottles and twisting the caps off before handing them to her.

"Thanks lovely! Oh, I heard your boys will be in town tomorrow night," she says, giving me a slight wiggle with her perfectly shaped eyebrows.

"Who told you that?" I ask, sounding a little defensive.

"Joey called me last night. I think he wants to start things up again," she replies, sounding less than enthusiastic and I can tell she was trying to read my reaction.

"Yeah." I looked at her straight on. "Does he have a shot?" I knew Jenna and Joey were hot and heavy during our senior year. It was a big deal then because Joey had already graduated and everyone thought he was sticking around for Jenna. She received a lot of attention for this and not always the good kind. I also knew Stone continuously gave Joey shit about being 'wifed up'.

"Fuck no," she replies, pushing her long blonde braid over her shoulder. "He broke up with me right before summer so he could 'pursue his career'. They fucking went to Vegas for the summer and you know he only wanted to be single. Besides, I'm kinda crushing on Logan right now." She smiles mischievously before walking away to deliver her table's beers.

I smirk. Joey was going to be so pissed to learn Jenna had a thing for Logan. He had been after her since freshman year and they were always just friends. If the guys were coming back tomorrow, things were going to get interesting again. I'd be lying to myself if I said I wasn't a little excited. I really needed a distraction. I probably just needed to get really drunk.

"Ooh, never mind Logan, I'll take the customer at table

seventeen," Jenna says, returning to the bar and pointing to her booth across the restaurant.

All I could see was what looked like a pretty solid shoulder covered by a tight black t-shirt. A muscled, bronze arm resting on the table, and a partial head of black hair poking out from behind the pillar. I shrug my shoulders at her and give her a wink for encouragement. Not that she needs it. Jenna is a master flirt. Laughing, she sauntered over to her new customer.

Talking with Jenna helped the night go by a little smoother. Some of the tension left my shoulders and my mind felt lighter. At least I wasn't pissing off Luis anymore. Behind the bar, I find it is easier to forget what's going on in my head. Every part of me was consumed with remembering tabs and ingredients. A few strawberry daiquiris, Dos Equis, cranberry vodkas, and Bud Lights later, my shift is almost over. In between her tables, Jenna would give me reports on her customer that she described as 'sex-on-a-stick', or 'if a love child between Wentworth Miller and Jack Gilinsky could happen'. Sadly, I haven't had an opportunity to confirm or deny her claims. All the other waitresses were in agreement with her though. Everyone was trying to sneak a peek at the visitor, making extra trips to my bar in order to walk past his booth.

I was determined to believe that men were probably not what I should be concerned with right now anyway. The few I have trusted in my life were not in my good graces lately. Besides, I had enough personal shit to deal with, I wouldn't even consider myself a good catch right now.

Looks-wise I was fine, but nothing substantial. Medium height, long black hair, a slightly curvy figure, not the reed-thin model types usually walking around the Vegas area, and my C-cup chest was indeed real. Blake had always told me I looked extraordinary because of my eyes. We shared the same icy blue hue outlined by a teal that couldn't be considered green or hazel. Unique, is how Seth described them the first time he tried to pay me a compliment. Blake, on the other hand, used these eyes to his advantage. Girls always seemed to go crazy over them. He never could understand why I usually downplayed my eyes by using dark eyeliner, deepening the color so they didn't pop out at anyone.

In all honesty, I thought the color was too intense and if anyone looked too long, then it would feel as if they were reading me. Crazy as the notion was, I took notice several times that the guys couldn't hold my gaze for long; proving me right. Yup, personal shit to deal with.

"Jenna, what are you doing tonight?" I ask her without thinking. Judging from the freaked out look on her face, I could tell it had been a while since I had reached out to her for anything besides work.

"Seriously?" she asked, her mouth opening in surprise.

"Oh my god. Never mind, if you're going to act all weird about it," I say, rolling my eyes. Stupid plan to step out of my bubble anyway.

"Blaise, I have been asking you to do things for months and you always turn me down to go home and sleep. I know you're dealing with shit and I haven't pressed, but I stopped asking because I just assumed you didn't care anymore," Jenna said quietly.

I guess I may have been a shittier friend than I thought. When the guys left, I took it too much to heart that I forgot about Jenna. Unlike my ex-friends, Zoe and Tara, who left for college without a word to me. Jenna was here and she was right, she did check on me. I didn't like the guilt that was flowing in my stomach even if I didn't feel like I owed anyone an explanation for my behavior.

"I screwed up," I tell her, biting my lip. "I'm screwed up. If there is anything going on tonight, I would like to go with you guys." That was as close to an apology as I could manage right now.

"Well, Aubree and Molly are coming, too. Will that be okay or is it too many people for you?" She gives me a pointed look with her eyebrows arched again. She must practice that.

Apparently, I haven't been as transparent with her as I thought I had been. Until a few months ago, being in large crowds would give me panicky chills. I also didn't go out of my way to meet people who could leave after I had gotten to know them. Which is why I barely knew the two new additions to Señor Loco's serving team.

"Yeah, that's fine. They seem decent," I reply, keeping my eyes on the mug I was drying and hoping my hands don't shake.

"Whatever, Blaise." I could hear the eye roll in her voice. "Anyway, new order for ya. Hottie McHotterson would like a Jameson on the rocks, please."

Now, it was my turn to raise my eyebrows at her. Rarely did anyone order straight liquor around here unless it was a shot of tequila.

"I know," she says, her smile growing bigger like the Cheshire Cat. "He wanted a Guinness, but we don't sell that here so he settled for the whiskey."

I stopped mid-scoop of ice in the glass. Guinness… Jameson… Irish beer, Irish Whiskey, Sarge's words play over in my head like a broken record. This was all either a coincidence or else I had just heard my Irish calling. My head snaps up, my eyes zeroing on her table. As if he knows I'm looking for him, his forearm tightens, veins and muscles ripple under the skin.

"Blaise?" Jenna asks, looking at me like I've grown two heads. I was too busy concentrating on her customer to answer. That stupid pillar was in the way and I wanted to see more of him. Something felt familiar, the longer I stared, until a small tidal wave of heat was growing in my chest.

"Here," I say, feeling uneasy, handing her his whiskey on the rocks. She eyes me before walking away heading to his table. Drying a glass, I watch Jenna approach him. She sets her hand on her hip and smiles when she sets the glass down, lingering longer than normal. He asks her something, and she chats away in response. I was being ridiculous, practically stalking them. I really need to have another conversation with Sarge about this before it totally interrupts my life. Before I do something like go over and ask him if he was sent to deliver a cryptic message for me. That wouldn't seem crazy at all.

Looking back at the table, I see him getting up to leave. A black leather jacket setting across his broad back. He was tall. I was average height and from this distance, he looked like he was at least a foot taller than me.

"Shit!" Jenna says under her breath. "I hope he paid, I never brought him his bill." She hurries away from the bar back to his table, her tray sloshing freshly poured beer as she goes. Without hesitating, I round the bar to follow after Mr. Tall, Mysterious, and possible Bill Skipper. He didn't get far out of the door before I catch up to him in the parking lot.

"Hey!" I shout to his retreating back. He stops automatically. "Did you forget something back there?" I ask. His bill, or to deliver a message to me, I wasn't sure which I was referring to. I watch in fascination when he turns to face me. Time seems to go in slow motion. My gaze flies over his dark washed jeans and the tight black shirt that's pulled tight against his chest. I greedily take in the dark, five o'clock shadow around his square cut jaw and full pink lips, before traveling upward to meet his eyes.

The second our gazes lock, recognition rockets through my brain. I was looking into the deepest, rich, brown gaze I have only ever seen once before. I quickly look down at my feet breaking eye contact. My face burns bright red with embarrassment and I'm suddenly thankful for the dimness of the parking lot. Memories from that night flood in. The pain, the funeral, the emptiness, and finally the stranger who had made me feel whole and protected while he fucked me against a bathroom wall.

"Blaise!" Jenna yells from the door. "It's okay, it was on the table." I turn to her and give her a sharp nod. A deep laugh comes from the man behind me. I turn back to face him again, my face completely red now, I'm sure. I can't believe I chased him out here and was about to accuse him of walking out on his bill.

"Sorry," I mumble, not able to look at his face. I start to back up and head back into the restaurant, anxious to be away from him.

"I would never walk out on my tab," he tells me. His smooth voice sends ripples of awareness across my chest. It's achingly familiar, and that accent is still as sexy as it was back then.

"She wasn't sure," I answer back, wringing the towel in my hands. "We don't get many people from out of town here." The excuse sounds lame even to me, but I hope he buys it. Frickin' Jenna should have checked first. No, I should have waited for her to confirm before chasing after him.

"That's understandable," he says, his voice holds humor in it like he can see right through me.

"Okay, well… have a good night," I tell him, taking a few more steps back to safety. I need to be back in the bar and far away from him. I remember him, but there was no recognition in his eyes when he looks at me. He was probably a wreck that night and drunk out of his mind to have sex with a random girl in a bar. Especially when that girl had looked like a cold, crying, drowned mess.

I almost reach the door when his next words stop me in my tracks. "I'm here for you, Blaise."

My eyes close and I make my body turn back around to face him. "Irish?" I ask, not believing this is real. Fate had to be messing with me right now.

"Just a joke." His massive shoulders shrug. "Makes it easier for introductions and it's more fun." A crooked grin plays on his lips. At least one of us thinks this is funny.

"Okay," I say. I'm not sure where this is all going or why this all seems so intense and secretive. "So you have information about my brother?" I ask, getting straight to the point. I was done playing the game. His game, Sarge's game, Seth's game, Blake's game. I was just done.

He stalks closer to me, my head tilts back to hold eye contact, "We're getting an audience, do you work tomorrow?" he asks, lowering his voice. He's so close I can smell the spearmint gum hidden in his cheek mixing with the whiskey he drank.

I should be disturbed by his nearness. I should back up into my own bubble again. Unfortunately, my brain and my body has decided to take a vacation from one another. I don't want him to know my schedule and think he can start showing up at my work, but the words "At four," fall out of my mouth anyway.

"Good," he says, still grinning at me with those dark, piercing eyes hiding secrets. "I'm working at Sergeant Ramirez's ranch in the morning. Drop by and we can talk more." It isn't a question, more like a command and my stupid head nods in agreement anyway. Without looking back, he turns and walks away.

"Don't you want to know if Seth has contacted me?" I ask, folding my arms across my chest waiting for his reaction.

"Blaise, that question just told me he hasn't. If he does, ask him where he is." Leaving me speechless, I watch Mr. Mysterious get in his black truck and peel out of my parking lot. A small dust cloud forms in his wake.

I'm completely overwhelmed when I head back in and sure enough, Jenna and Luis are guarding the door.

"What did McHottie say?" Jenna pounces the minute I step inside. At least my one and only fling had been drop dead gorgeous. It irked me though that he didn't remember me and now he had secretive information about my brother.

"He was upset I accused him of skipping out," I lie.

"Oh," she says. "I hope you didn't put him off of coming here again, Blaise, you can be kind of brassy sometimes."

"Brassy?" I ask, narrowing my eyes.

"I'm sorry," she says, shaking her head and smiling. "It's true though. I think you scare Luis sometimes even."

"It's fine. I have my moments. I think he'll be back though," I say, giving her a little wink. If something serious was going on, I didn't want to be tied to him. Better to let her think he would come back to see her. Too bad for Logan.

"Oh, the party got moved to tomorrow night now. I guess Marco heard Toni would be back and decided to wait for them." Jenna shrugs her shoulders. I already forgot I had agreed to go to the party.

I smile at her, hiding my annoyance with myself. "Okay, sounds good."

By the end of the night, I'm thankful to be able to crawl into my bed instead. My body hurts from carrying trays and my brain was exhausted from trying to piece together this game I landed myself in. I fall asleep still contemplating if I should reach out to Seth or if that would be bad for myself. There were too many pieces that weren't lining up. I didn't know who to trust. Someone was underestimating me, I could feel it.

Four

MY EYES FLY OPEN, MY HEART IS hammering in my chest as I'm startled awake. I quickly look around my room from the cocoon of my blankets. Something woke me up. My skin feels tingly as gooseflesh works its way over my arms. Holding my breath, I listen. Did my mom come home or was someone trying to break in? Six a.m shines brightly on the clock from my nightstand. I hunch farther back in my covers, waiting.

Tap. Tap. Tap.

I throw my blankets off and face my window. A shadow outlined by the early morning sky greets me. I inch closer, feeling uncertain, my breath grows shallow as I move closer to the curtain.

Tap. Tap. Tap.

Jerking the curtains apart, I'm surprised to see Joey laughing at me. "What the hell?" I ask, opening my window.

"I'm sorry," he gasps between laughs. "Your face though!"

"Yeah, yeah." I move to shut the window. It was too damn early to deal with this shit.

His hand shoots out. "I'm sorry, Blaise. You just looked so freaked out. Were you expecting someone?"

"Yeah, I was expecting someone at six in the morning, Chuckles. What are you doing here?" I ask, folding my arms over my chest as I sit at my desk chair. Seth's face flashes in my mind. Joey is already moving his stocky body through my window before sitting across from me on the bed.

"Geez, Toni said you were upset, but I didn't realize it was this bad," he says, watching me intently.

I look away from his blue gaze. My eyes sting from the emotion in my chest. "I'm fine," I tell him. "Back to my question, why are you here at six in the morning? This little pep talk couldn't wait till decent hours?" I ask. I'm beyond curious and I hate that I'm also excited he clearly came here first before going home. His shirt was wrinkled from a long car ride.

I hear him exhale. "I just wanted to make sure your mom wasn't around before I came up."

"Couldn't use the front door?" I let the sarcasm roll off my tongue, finally turning to look at him. He shrugs, a lopsided smile pulling at his mouth. I frown.

"We're back in town and just wanted to check up on you. It's been a minute. Your mom isn't home anyway," he states.

"Yeah, well she's been picking up extra shifts, something about it helping her heal. And, I knew you were coming back. Jenna said she talked to you," I say, letting my voice sound bored.

"Jenna, aye? Can't wait to see that hottie tonight." His grin grows bigger.

"I don't know, she's been pretty tight with Logan this summer,"

I tell him, watching his smile fade a little before he lets out a high pitched laugh.

"Anyway, there's a party tonight at Marco's. Just wanted to say you should come. We'd all love to see you. Stone said to let him know when you get there," Joey says, leaning forward to meet my eyes.

"I was already invited. I don't really party anymore though. You can tell Stone and the others 'Hi' and I'll see them around, during decent hours," I add and Joey laughs again. The sound warms me a little. I forgot how much these guys don't take anything seriously, so I raise my eyebrow at him.

"Okay," he says, holding his hands up in surrender. "I gotta get back and catch some sleep anyway." He turns to leave and I follow him back to the window. "I'll see you later, Blaisy." He reaches out and tugs on my top-knot.

"See you, Joe," I reply, holding the window until he was out on the balcony again.

"Oh, I almost forgot." He turns back to me. "Just wondering, have you heard from Seth since the funeral? I can't get ahold of him."

My heart stops before kicking into overdrive. My face contorted in anger. "Seriously? Have I heard from Seth? I haven't heard from anyone since the funeral. I thought you all were on vacation in Vegas gambling, sleeping around, and partying. No, I haven't heard from Seth."

"Okay," he says quietly, looking around to see if any of my neighbors woke up. "Blaise, I'm sorry. There was just no way to hang out around here after. We should have called you though." He rakes a hand through the blonde mess on his head.

I let out a breath I didn't realize I was holding and shrug. "I don't know what to say."

"Hope I see you later," he answers, tugging my knot again in goodbye. My head jerks in response. I watch him in a daze as he climbs down the stairs and gets on his bike that's parked in front of the building.

The sun is just starting to come up over the horizon. A haze was forming, indicating that it was going to be another hot day. I close the window and bury myself back in my blankets. More questions flood my mind. I squeeze my eyes tight attempting to block out everything. Frustrated, I roll onto my back and stare at the ceiling. I try to relax my body but my nerves were strung tight. At this point, falling back asleep was not going to happen. Looking at the clock, it was now seven. Might as well get up.

THE DIRT ROAD to Sarge's seemed to go on forever. My stomach is twisted in knots over seeing Mr. Mysterious again. I want answers about as much as I want to turn, hightail it back to town, and just hide in bed until my shift starts. I believe Sarge wouldn't be helping unless he also thought something was up with the case. It was hard to blindly trust Mr. Mysterious though. I don't really know him. Only that he had incredible eyes and was very talented with a few of his extremities. I shake my head, clearing those thoughts. He obviously doesn't remember. It would be better for me in the long run for him not to find out.

As I round the last curve, I immediately see his big black truck that had peeled out of the parking lot last night. He was already here. A few chills ran down my back and the butterflies in my stomach take off again. It was stupid getting so worked up like this. I park next to Sarge's squad car like I always do before unclasping my seatbelt and getting out. Pricilla sees me from in the house and waves. I give her a little wave back before I start walking toward the stable area.

Sarge is loading up the bed of his work truck with stacks of hay. Mr. Mysterious is helping to pile everything on top. He stops when he sees me, his gaze raking down my body from head to foot. I feel him taking in my destroyed jean shorts, vintage AC/DC t-shirt and grey Chucks. A blush spreads across my cheeks. I turn to Sarge first and spread a fake smile across my face to go with my small wave. Sarge hugs me while Mr. Sexy Eyes hops down from the truck. He peels off his gloves and drinks from his water bottle, his eyes still intently on me.

"Glad you could make it, Blaise," Sarge says to me.

I shrug in response. "Wouldn't miss this for the world." Sarge turns to me, his mouth set in a grim line. "This here is Detective McCall from Las Vegas. He's the one who has some information on Blake."

"We met unofficially," Detective McCall informs him. My blush deepens, thinking he is referring to our first meeting. "I ran into Blaise at Señor Loco last night," he says and I let my breath out. He still thinks he met me for the first time last night. I want to laugh and at the same time, I want to stick my head in the sand.

"Jay," he says, holding out his large hand to me.

"Hi," I say before sliding mine into his. His long fingers tighten, sending shocks of awareness through me. Even in the arid ninety-degree heat, my hand feels cold inside his. I will myself to calm down and concentrate on the information this guy has.

"I'll leave you two to get caught up then so we can decide our next move," Sarge says, excusing himself. He hops in his truck and drives up toward the house. I watch Jay closely as his eyes follow Sarge's retreating form go inside.

"Want to take a walk?" he asks suddenly.

Again, I shrug. "Sure." We follow the path that takes us farthest from the house and I knew would eventually lead to a small swimming pond. Silence stretches between us the whole way down. *How was the sex for you? Why are you investigating my brother's death?* The questions linger on my tongue. I stay quiet, hoping he'll break the silence soon instead. He seems to like doing things his own way. When we get to the lake, I sit on the log bench that is still there. After a few seconds, he joins me. He leans back, letting his long legs stretch out. The movement caused his shirt to ride up, giving me a glimpse of tanned, smooth skin underneath. I quickly avert my eyes toward the water hoping he didn't notice me check him out.

"Not to be demanding or anything, but what is this all about?" I ask. I need a distraction.

"Not demanding, huh?" He smiles.

"No offense, but I sort of had plans I gave up before work to meet with you instead," I lie, picking at the polish on my nails.

His lips tilt in that knowing smirk. "It's a really long story, Blaise, there is no way I could have told you everything last night. I don't even know everything." His face hardens and he leans forward, cracking his knuckles.

"Why don't you tell me what you do know then. Why are you investigating my brother?" I don't care that I am demanding this time.

He's quiet for a moment, gazing out at the water. I see his throat bob and feel his body tense next to me.

"It's not really that simple, Blaise," he sighs. "I'm not investigating your brother. I'm investigating the events that led to his death. Blake didn't die in an accident."

His words run through my head, not making sense. "What?" I ask, my voice cracking.

"Listen, there is a lot you don't know about what happened back then that might make more sense now. There are also a lot of things I'm going to tell you that you won't believe, but I need you to trust me. What I'm going to tell you is the honest truth. I need to solve this case to find peace. For him to rest easily."

"Why would I trust you?" I ask.

"Blake did," he replies and just like that, he has my full attention.

"Start at the beginning, Jay," I whisper, pulling my knees up to my chest, I wrap myself up, holding together my insides and pushing back the sobs wanting to break free.

"I knew Blake for a few years. I made a huge drug bust awhile back which led me to a specific crew working in Las Vegas. Some bad shit happened one night and the next thing I knew Blake was in my office spilling all this vital information, fully cooperating. He began working with my team and me. Trading information for money. He said he had a younger sister who wanted to go to college. We worked together for about two years building the case. He became like a younger brother and friend to me." Jay stops talking, looking sideways at me intently, watching my expression. I stare back at him, wanting him to continue talking about Blake.

"A couple weeks before the accident, we began looking at a new angle on the case. It really upset your brother, but he was all in to keep helping us. He brought a friend in—"

"Seth," I say, not even having to guess at this point.

"Yeah, and things took a sideways turn from there," he answers.

"How?" I ask him. The story couldn't end there and again, why is Seth in the middle of this.

"We have no idea what happened. There was a solid plan in place. We walked through every detail many times and we designated which hotel everything would go down at. I wasn't going to be in Vegas with them that night. I was doing surveillance on another piece of important detail in case things did go bad. The whole plan was flawless. Somehow though, Blake ended up almost here, he was dead and a bag of money went missing along with your friend," Jay explains, shaking his head.

"Are you saying Seth was responsible for the car accident?" I practically shouted before standing up to pace back and forth. I could feel Jay watching me, anticipating my next actions, expecting an outburst. "That doesn't even make sense! They were best friends. Blake drove fast all the time. He was reckless on more than one occasion."

"Blaise…" Jay says softly, standing up in front of me before placing his hands on my shoulders, stopping my movement, "The coroner's report showed that he had a fatal amount of heroin in his system. He died before the car even hit that tree."

"Are you fucking kidding me? Blake did not do drugs!" My heart was racing. None of what Jay was telling me made any sense. "He wouldn't even smoke marijuana! He hated drugs so much because of our dad. What about my mom? Why didn't we know this before? Shouldn't someone have told us back then that he was murdered instead of us believing it was a pointless, stupid accident?"

Jay lets a breath out, his hands scraping over the scruff on his jaw. "We couldn't let details out because the investigation is still open. Believe me, I would have told you sooner if I could have. I'm only allowed to now after being sent here. It's been months and the fuckers responsible haven't been tagged yet and the bag is still missing. All of our concrete evidence is in that bag."

"So, now what?" I ask. I can feel the sting of tears behind my eyes. The last thing I want to do is cry in front of Jay. I just need to run and turn off my mind.

"We wait. I need to find Seth. Blake's last call was an incoming one from Seth. Blaise, I need that bag to help this case," Jay answers.

"What do you need from me?" The words fall quietly out of my mouth. I figure this must be the main point of him being here. This is the reason for the secrets and the games. Why else go to the sister and not the parents.

Jay takes my hands in his, turning me to face him. "I need you to pretend I'm new in town and just helping Sergeant Ramirez working part-time at the ranch. We never had this conversation. Just act like we're friends." I accidentally snort rolling my eyes. His beautiful ones narrow at me. "Can't be my friend, Blaise?"

"We hardly know each other. I'm not very friendly these days to the people I do consider friends," I warn him. No one was about to believe I just happened to thaw from an ice queen and picked up a new friend within days.

"I wouldn't say we hardly know each other," he says, taking a step closer to me. My face flames bright red, and my chest flares with anxiety.

"What about Seth?" I change the subject before he says anything else. A small bubble of hope that maybe he did remember that night forms. The thought makes me super uncomfortable.

He laughs, clearly aware of my embarrassment. "If you hear from Baird, just let me know. I need to find out where he is."

"What about my mom?" I ask. Testing him to see how well he really knew Blake.

He studies my face before crossing his arms across his chest. "Blake wouldn't have gone to her. There is nothing she would know more about than you. When this is all over, I'll tell her what really happened to him.."

"Fine," I say, pulling back from him. "The only reason I'm not calling bullshit right now is because Sarge approves of you."

"I would expect nothing less of you, Blaise," he answers, watching me retreat back up the hill. "I'll see you tonight," he says, the words were so quiet I barely hear them as I make my way back to the ranch. I run the rest of the way to my car, jump in and tak off down the dirt road.

So many things Jay told me didn't make sense, yet in a weird way, I believe him. Part of me knows Blake was a crazy driver, but he always handled himself. I knew he had been extra busy lately, but I attributed it to the Vegas lifestyle. He had encouraged me to stay home and study for the ACT instead of coming with him during spring break. I thought he just wanted me to do good so I could get into any college I wanted. Now I was doubting anything my brother had ever told me. The Blake that Jay was describing to me was not the same person I thought I knew.

The tears I had been holding back coast down my cheeks freely, my heart squeezes in pain. He had made a plan for himself and for me. My older brother always put me before himself and this time it may have cost him his life. Guilt eats at my stomach when I finally arrive home. The apartment was dark, and I could tell my mom wasn't home again. With only a few hours left until my shift, I decide to run. I need the connection and the burn in my lungs to help erase the feelings in my heart.

Five

AFTER MY FIVE-MILE RUN, I decided to go into work early. Luis accepts my help and one of the new servers is relieved to go home early. Usually, I don't like serving. I prefer to be busy behind the bar so that time goes by faster. Tonight though, I just need my mind focused on anything except the conversation with Jay, err-Detective McCall. Taking orders and having to be polite to random strangers seems like a good way to do that.

I was being honest when I told him I hadn't heard from Seth. No matter how hard I try to ignore it, I feel guilty thinking I may have to rat on Seth. All these mixed feelings swirling in my head were giving me a headache. I almost hope I never hear from the kid again. It's painful to imagine a person I have known forever, *my first…* could somehow be connected to Blake's murder. That's what it was now. Murder. Not an accident. I shudder.

A few mind-numbing hours later, I'm on my way to Jenna's

before the party. My plan had been to just go to the party, but she made a big deal about us girls getting ready together. I suddenly missed hanging out with guys. They didn't care about that stuff and neither did I.

I pull up to her house and can hear the latest pop hits blaring from inside. Two other cars are also on the driveway, so I assume the other girls are already here. Before I can knock, Logan opens the door, dipping into an overly gallant pose and ushers me in.

"Girls are upstairs," he says, taking a sip of the beer in his hand.

"Are you just on door duty?" I ask him, laughing.

"It's better than hearing about bra straps, cat eyes, and which heels match better," he answers, rolling his eyes. I nod my head, agreeing with him one hundred percent. The thought of going upstairs makes my insides curl. Looking down, I study the basic strappy sandals I had put on earlier. Definitely not high heels or even the latest fashion trend.

"Anyway, Jenna's pretty excited you're coming tonight, you should head up there," Logan tells me, interrupting my thoughts.

I take the stairs slowly, hoping to avoid the rest of Justin Bieber's "Sorry." I can still hear Logan chuckling as he goes back into the safety of the kitchen. The minute I reach her room, Jenna is on me.

"Blaise!" she yells, flinging her arms around my shoulders. "It's about time, I thought you were backing out. Want some 'strip and go naked'?" she asks, passing me a large-sized drink cooler.

"Started early?" I ask, taking the jug and holding it away from my nose. The smell is strong and sour. "What's in it?"

"Vodka, pink lemonade, and beer," the girl with the bobbed black hair lists off for me. I think her name is Molly. She stands up swiftly on her towering wedge heels, her jean skirt making her normally short legs look a mile long before she walks over to us.

I peek quickly down at my jeans. I was proud that I had found a pair that had some sparkles and still fit me pretty well. After Blake died and the guys moved, I never went out. Basic black jeans and shorts were all I owned. My tops were all tanks, old band t-shirts, one camouflage and one black leather jacket were my go-to.

"Blaise, are you going to change?" Jenna asks me and I frown.

"Umm, I was just going to wear this," I say, taking a quick pull from the jug. The bitterness from the lemonade makes my lips pucker. Judging by the looks on the girls' faces, I guess that the dress code at Marco's must have changed since I was there last.

"Don't be silly," Jenna says, throwing a piece of white denim at me. "You can borrow mine. But I want it back." She winks.

I walk into her bathroom and shut the door before stripping off my jeans. The skirt hugs me perfectly, and of course, was provocatively short. I pull the ends down, turning in the mirror to make sure my ass is covered. I don't mind letting skin show and would never tell a girl she had to cover it up. As long as I wasn't bending over for anything tonight, I'll be fine. Opening the bathroom door, Jenna stands right in front of me, holding out a scrap of bubblegum pink material. That's where I draw the line.

"I'm good with this," I tell her, gesturing to my thin strap, black tank I threw on earlier. She rolls her eyes. "Fine," Jenna says before her hand reaches out and snatches the hair tie at the end of my braid, letting it loose. My hair now hanging around my shoulders in messy waves.

"Perfect!" the other blonde, Aubree I think, slurs slightly, clapping her hands together.

My eyebrow arches. "We should go," I say, directing them toward the door. If we stay here any longer, these girls will have to be carried to the party.

Marco's parents' house is off another long dirt road hidden from prying eyes making it the perfect house for his notorious parties. It also helped that his parents worked full time and often were gone on the weekends. Marco was a year younger than me in school, but it didn't stop his reputation for having the best house to drink, hook up, and smoke some weed. The guys and I had been going to Marco's parties since his freshman year in high school. Each year the party grew bigger and each year he found a way to top what he did previously.

We pulled up in Logan's Jeep. People were already pouring in from every direction. Beer pong was set up in the front yard next to a half-mile long slip-n-slide that sent participants into the pool out back. Meek Mill's "House Party" was on blast inside the house. I grin as the beat pulses through my body. Roxy was set up to DJ tonight so everyone would be dancing. She was the only one I knew who actually could mix a rock song with some rap and vice versa. Somehow she always made it work.

Inside the home, a slight haze hung in the air and the furniture was pushed against the wall leaving space for the dance floor. A few kegs were lined up to the side, while bodies moved from room to room. In the back of the house, a pool table sat and I knew that's where I would find the guys if they were here. Joey had said they would be, but as usual they hadn't said anything to me all day. I hesitate to walk back there even though part of me wants to show them I couldn't care less if they were home, just like they couldn't have cared less all summer that I was here by myself.

Instead, I let Jenna pull me over to the kegs. Weaving through the crowd, I earn a few head nods and I recognize some of the people from my grade that just graduated. Yup, everyone comes back for a Marco party. With our cups full, I listen to the girls talk about the different boys they want to hook up with. I make sure to nod and grin where acceptable. All the while, I can't help scanning the crowd.

I easily spot Roxy's purple fauxhawk, bobbing in time to Des Rocs' "Let Me Live/Let Me Die" that she was mixing in. The crowd was loving it. I find Marco standing close to the DJ table as well, and lift my glass in salute. He smiles and gives me a nod before turning back to the person on his left. My eyes shift and I do a double take. Marco's head is tilted toward Detective McCall. He hasn't noticed me yet so I use this time to let my eyes wander over Jay. He looks casual and delicious at the same time. His denim jeans hang low on his hips, a plain white T-shirt stretches across his broad chest and ends just a hair below his belt line. His closely cropped hair is covered in a backward navy blue NVU baseball hat with a flat bill. As my eyes rake him up and down, they touch briefly on the silver dog tags hanging from his neck. Everything about Jay causes my blood to heat. An energy runs through my veins and I bite my lip to keep in the moan I want to release just from looking at him. My eyes are caught by Marco, who's now looking from Jay to me. I turn away, my cheeks flushing pink. How were Marco and Jay connected already?

I don't have time to think about it before a strong arm lands around my shoulders, and I'm turned into Joey's side. His button-down shirt is open showing off his lean frame under his white muscle tank with his blond hair gelled in spikes over the top of his head. With his arm around me he wolfishly smiles at Jenna who had been separated from Logan when we got in the house.

"Hey Blaise," he says, giving me a small peck on the side of my head. "Hey ladies."

"Hi Joey," Jenna responds, lifting her chin a notch. She was not going to let him walk all over her for once. I like that she was giving

Joey a hard time. He needed a taste of his own medicine sometimes. Using my elbow, I give Joey a shove in the side.

"Ahh," he says laughing, his arm dropping to grab my hand. "Guys want to say hello," he tells me, turning so we're face to face, his head inclines toward the back. My skin prickles with awareness. My eyes slide over Joey's shoulder, my gaze colliding with Jay's. He's watching me intently despite the busty blonde who was now grinding against his dick like she was trying to get off. I snap my eyes back to Joey.

"Okay," I say, shrugging my shoulders. I can't fight the irritation that was crawling up my throat from seeing Jay and that chick. It's not like we are together. We had only been together once and only one of us seemed to remember. His idea from yesterday that we should be friends seemed far-fetched when neither of us was making moves to even look friendly.

"Later ladies," Joey announces before tugging me behind him through the crowd. People part to let us pass. The hall becomes darker the farther away from the main room we get while verses from Kid Rock's "Cowboy" float in the air. I hear the clang of the pool balls bouncing against each other before we reach the alcove, causing my heart to speed up. Rounding the corner, a small group hovers around a pool table, behind them, I see the top of Stone's head.

At six feet four inches, he was always a little taller than the other guys. His jet black hair, normally shoulder length, was pulled in a bun. Dressed in all black, he was an intense sight. Antonio, his cousin, sat in a chair with a redhead in his lap who was dressed to the nines and not for a house party. Even though Stone and Antonio were related, their personalities are complete opposites. Toni is the jokester who is always easy going and he functions best after hitting a bowl. His hair is kept short with buzzed designs on the sides. Toni also prefers to wear as little as possible. Even now, he wore a pair of jeans with no shirt and flip-flops. His tattoos are visible to everyone, and that's how he likes it, is my guess. Stone radiated control and dominance. It was rare he smiled, but when he did, it was blinding. Many women fall for the smile, but they never last longer than a week. Same for all these guys, except Joey, and they never let him forget he was pussy whipped. All their personalities balance each other out. Only now they were missing two in the group.

When they finally see me, Toni jumps up first, his date glaring at me from the ground where she lands. "Blaisy!" he yells before grabbing me up in a huge hug and spinning me around.

"Whoa." I laugh, slapping his shoulders to set me back down.

"Sorry, little Palmer, just missed you," he says. His voice was drawn out, and I could tell he already had a few hits tonight. His eyes are glassy as he smiles at me.

"Still could have called," I tell him, ignoring the way his smile falls.

"We all should have called," Stone's deep voice echoes behind us. We turn to look at him. Toni sits back down, pulling his friend back into his lap. Joey stands off to the side watching. His gaze slides between us and the game at the pool table.

"Would have been nice," I reply, meeting Stone's grey eyes. He looks me over before nodding his head.

"Does it help if we say it was hard on us to lose Blake, too?" he asks. Blake's name rolling off his tongue sends a jolt of pain through my heart. I keep eye contact, trying to read him. As usual, Stone is closed off, his face a mask, giving nothing away.

"I missed you," I finally say, looking around at all three of them. Joey and Antonio both nod in agreement while looking at the floor. Emotions are not their favorite thing and this situation was getting group hug worthy.

"Well, we're back now," Stone says, stepping closer to me. Our chests were almost touching. I realize this was the most physical contact I'd had with him since we were kids. There was something about Stone that screamed danger. I was never sure if it was because he was older than us or because he always was so guarded, but I could never understand him, never could figure out his next move. Right now, I had to fight the urge to take a step back, feeling like I'd lose some undeclared battle if I did.

Before he could say anything else, Molly and Jenna run in grabbing my arms. "Blaise! C'mon, it's our song, let's shake our asses!" Jenna yells as they usher me away. I look back and all three were on their feet watching me. Ignoring the chills zipping across my skin, I smile and wave hoping it eases the tension of us being interrupted. Secretly, I was happy to go to the dance floor. This night was one surprise after another, and I need to get the anxiety and resentment out of my system.

I quickly chug the beer I have left and feel it burn my chest as it goes down. It has been a while since I partied. The two drinks already are making me feel light and tipsy. Jenna tugs me to the middle of the dance floor where Aubree was already grinding on one guy. My hips find the rhythm in Ty Dolla $ign's "Paranoid," and soon all the crap from earlier leaves my head and I live in the moment. Something I haven't done for months.

I almost lost my footing when two strong hands find my hips and pulls my body back, right into a strong wall. Without looking, I know it's Jay holding me. He smells like fresh air, mint gum and a hint of beer. His body surrounds me and I lean into him, absorbing the feel of him. His hips move against mine seductively causing shivers to run up my arms despite the warmth in the room. The feeling is similar to the first time we met. I stiffen slightly at the thought.

Sensing the change, he bends his head down until his chin rests on my shoulder, the bill of his hat rubbing against my hair.

"Don't think," he whispers into my ear. I smile and decide he's right. I don't want to think. There is no harm in enjoying his muscled arms around my waist and following his lead to the music. Before I close my eyes, giving in completely, I spot Stone and Joey watching me from the shadow of the hallway. Once meeting my eyes, they both turn and walk away to the backroom.

"Good job, Blaise," Jay murmurs against the side of my neck, sending tingles flying down my body. I turn to look at him, confused, instead he pulls me tighter to him. I'll probably have fingertip bruises on my sides from where he grips me, and strangely the idea is appealing. My buzz relaxes me even when warning bells are trying to signal my brain. Jay is warm and holds me together. I decide to ignore everything else.

Six

A SOFT FEMININE SNORE WAKES me up. Through the dark blinds, the sun is visible, causing my eyes to water before grimacing in pain. Red numbers from the clock across the room reads nine a.m. My head is pounding from the last few shots the girls had insisted we do at Marco's. I shift myself up on my elbows and notice I'm in Jenna's room on the futon. Aubree and Jenna are lying the long way across the bed in various disarray in their clothes from last night and yoga pajama pants. I have no idea where Molly is. Vague images of her deciding to go with a guy from the party, float in my memory. I frown.

I gingerly push myself to a sitting position before going into Jenna's bathroom to freshen up. My eyes lock on the mirror, I sweep a hand threw my hair before realizing there was no helping this mess. I groan, leaning my head against my reflection as I run some cold water in the sink. I quickly doused my face with water and swish some in my mouth, swallowing a little to help ease the sandpapery feel. I use a tissue to wipe the black eyeliner from under my eyes, hoping it makes me look less of a raccoon. It's all coming back to me, why I didn't miss going to parties.

The girls are still sleeping when I'm done, so I grab my jeans off the floor and leave the skirt Jenna had loaned me. Quietly, I sneak down the stairs only to find Logan waiting in the kitchen. "Breakfast is ready," he calls, waving at me with a spatula. I debate with myself if I really need to stay, before giving in and walking over to him. He piles eggs and bacon on a plate before handing it to me. I half expect my stomach to roll instead it growls in hunger.

"Wow," I say. "He chauffeurs and he cooks." Logan tilts his head back with a deep laugh.

"Anything for my girls," he replies, sending me a wink. I roll my eyes in response before sitting at the island and taking a few bites. The kid could cook.

"Good?" he asks.

"Mhmm." I nod my head, my mouth stuffed full.

"Glad you like it," he responds before going back to cracking more eggs in the pan. "Hey, who was that guy at Marco's last night?" he asks, turning to me.

I shrug at first. Do I tell Logan the story Jay had handed to me? I'm still not sure how believable it is. "I think he's working at Sarge's ranch part-time," I tell him, keeping my face blank, and thankful for the food in front of me so I can avoid eye contact.

"Oh," Logan says. "I thought he was fixing parts at Rowley's in town. Doesn't he live in the apartment above the garage?"

This was news to me. How close Jay was actually staying to my home for some reason gave me butterflies. I shrug again, not really sure how to answer. "Maybe."

"Maybe what?" Jenna asks, breezing into the kitchen. I'm pretty sure she drank more than me last night, yet somehow she looks completely refreshed, like she stepped out of a spa.

"The new guy at Marco's," Logan answers her.

"Oh! Hottie McHotterson!" she says, gushing over the nickname she gave Jay. I feel my cheeks heat.

"He's okay, I guess," Logan says, frowning at Jenna. She laughs before throwing her arms around his waist.

"Don't worry, baby," she reassures him. "I think you are very HOT, besides, I believe he is taken." Jenna looks at me pointedly, a slight smirk on her face.

"I don't know what you mean," I say, concentrating again on my food.

"You dirty danced with him all night!" Jenna practically yells, swishing her hips at the same time.

"We did not," I respond, rolling my eyes and keeping my voice neutral, trying to defend myself.

"Blaise," she says, pointing a finger at me. "He was all over you."

The image she conjures in my mind makes my blush deepen. The room feels warmer. I hadn't thought much about last night thanks to the beers and tequila. It had been fantastic and I knew I had been sad when Jay left our group early. It didn't cross my mind last night, but today I remember he left when Stone, Joey, and Antonio did.

"It was just dancing," I tell them, shoving the last piece of egg in my mouth. "I barely know him."

I need to remember Jay was here for a job. A job involving my brother's possible murder, no less. And he still doesn't remember me, but at this point, it was a good thing. There were too many blurred lines already. Even I knew Jay had to be in his mid-twenties and would probably freak if he knew he had randomly hooked up with a "just turned eighteen that day" girl. No, it was probably best if we didn't cross paths too often, unless it had to do with helping my brother's case. Sadly, even as my mind thinks the words, my heart speeds up and my body does that weird warm flush remembering how good he had felt against me last night.

"Well, thanks for breakfast and the hangover," I say to Jenna and Logan, offering a salute before leaving the kitchen. I need to be in my own space and let my head deflate a little.

Like always, the apartment is empty when I get home. A scribbled note is on the counter from my mom saying she has gone out of town with friends and would be back Monday. I make my way to my room and turn the fan on. Even in September, living in the desert has its hot days. Before I draw my blinds, I looked at the building adjacent to ours where Logan said Jay was staying. Those blinds were up too, but the place looks dark inside. Shrugging to myself, I swallow some Advil before I lay down and let the dark bliss take me.

I HAVEN'T SEEN Jay since the party. More than a week has passed. I know it shouldn't matter and I keep reminding myself why he was really here. The guys stop in regularly at Señor Locos to see me and their group of friends. Tonight, I recognize one of their friends as an ex running back from the neighboring town's football team. All of the girls flock to him, seeing as he is 'new meat'. It reminds me of Jenna and the other servers the night Jay first came to town.

I sigh, hating how my mind always seems to gravitate to Jay since the night of the party. It would be stupid of me to assume he felt the same electricity between us, but I was dying to know more about him. I wasn't going to lie, as much as I want to see him, I also want to know if anything new had come up in Blake's case. I dry another glass while deciding after my shift that I'll go to the apartment above the garage to find him. I was tired of waiting around.

"You almost done, Blaise?" Toni's voice breaks through my train of thought.

"Yup, just about," I respond, turning around to finish placing the clean glass on the rack.

"Want to go to Scar with us?" he asks, eyeing me hopefully. We haven't talked much since the party and I haven't actually hung out with the guys since they'd been back. Instead, I've been working and keeping to myself, skeptical of everyone and everything around me. Maybe I could use a break?

"Okay," I tell him, shrugging. Toni looks at me, surprised. "What?" I ask, arching my eyebrow daring him to say something. I know I'm not exactly Miss Personality these days, but no way is he allowed to comment.

"Nothing," he says, giving me his lazy smile. "Just will be nice to have everyone together since… well, you know…" His voice trails off, but his meaning isn't lost on me. It would be the first time we have all been together hanging out since before Blake died. Well, almost all of us.

No one has asked me about Seth lately and I still haven't heard from him. I constantly feel on edge about it. Having my mom gone for a few days didn't help. Not that she was a huge presence in my life, but the apartment felt eerily quiet, and goosebumps chase across my flesh when I feel as if I'm being watched, which was frequently.

"Yeah," I say, my voice is scratchy, swallowing around the lump in my throat. "So eleven, as usual?"

"You know it! I'll pick you up. Stone and Joey are going early to check out a car. They'll meet us there," he says while tapping the bar with his long index finger.

"Okay. I'm off at nine, I'll be ready." I nod.

"See you later, Blaisey," he says, throwing me a goofy smile over his shoulder. I smile and shake my head. I deserved to have some time with the guys. Maybe they will bring up Seth and then I can have some information for Jay. *Jay.*

"Get a grip, Palmer," I whisper to myself while mentally slapping my forehead.

Looking around the restaurant, I could see only a few booths were filled. The day had been dragging by slowly. I catch my reflection in the mirror over the bar, then decide that if I was going out tonight, I would definitely need some time to make myself look presentable. Fry grease and beer stains did not do anything for my complexion.

Before I can stop myself, I wonder if Jay will be there tonight. He seems to be running in the same circles as Marco and the guys. My stomach flip-flops thinking about seeing him while my head still reasons that I shouldn't care. Groaning in frustration, I lay my head on my arm and look at the clock before climbing on the stool to get the glasses I prepped for tomorrow. Only a few hours left.

Seven

B Y TEN P.M., I'M SHOWERED, my hair is dry. I attempted my makeup as best as I could and changed my outfit five times. Anxiety is dripping from my pores, and a flush creeps over my skin making sweat dot my upper lip. It was getting closer and closer to when Toni would be picking me up.

Pacing in front of my closet, I examine my outfit again. God, I was becoming one of those girls. I never used to have this problem. Blake would say it was time to go, and I just went, not caring what I looked like. I hated feeling this desperate need to please. The denim washed jeans I wore hugged my legs perfectly. They were ripped at the thighs showing the fishnet tights I had on underneath. A grey cut-off t-shirt that was cropped right below my black lace halter bra was covered by my army jacket. The black eyeliner I applied to my eyes made them look smokey, while the shimmer gloss I applied to my lips tinted them almost red.

At the last minute, I decided to leave my hair down in waves. I'm finally ready and have to hold a fist against my stomach to contain the waves rolling around. "Blaise!" I hear my name called, followed by a few knocks at the door. Toni was here. I leaped off my bed, quickly stepping into my black Converse on the way down the hall.

"Hey," I greet him, opening the door so he can step in before I head into the kitchen quickly to grab the spare key.

"Hey," he says, his voice trailing off when he looks around at the dark and quiet apartment.

"My mom is working tonight," I tell him, feeling like I need to explain why the apartment looks like it hasn't been lived in, even if it was a lie. For some reason, I don't want to just tell Toni that my mom took off for another girl's weekend. It feels personal. His eyes locked on Blake's senior picture on the opposite wall.

"Gotcha," he responds quietly, his eyes still on the picture. "We should go." He slips me the smile that I knew too well it usually meant Toni was up to something.

I follow Toni out to his car, a sleek, red Corvette Z06 race car that he frequently drove at Scar when they had been in high school. Toni was a great driver and had won many races back in the day. I knew Blake had bet on him more than a few times to win so that we had extra grocery money. Before my buckle even clicked into place, Crazy Town's "Butterfly" was bumping from the stereo. Unable to help myself, I laugh.

"What?" Toni asks, his voice mischievous, a huge grin pulling at his lips. "I'm bringing old school back." He starts to sing and I pretend to cringe at how off-key he is. We laugh and sing the song on repeat while he drives us out of town and toward the desert.

Scar is a dirt racing track located out of town out in the sand. It was out of Sarge's jurisdiction and belonged on a piece of reservation.

The cops didn't care about the gambling, illegal street races or the underage drinking. It was a haven for criminals and thrill-seekers. By the time we pulled up, the place was already packed and a few races were already going.

Toni slides his car up next to Joey's Jeep. Their friends are parked nearby, some sitting in truck beds, on lawn chairs, and on the hoods of cars. The atmosphere is filled with adrenaline. The air is thick with dust and the smell of burning rubber and gasoline. We walked over to where Stone and Joey are waiting, and I let my eyes scan the crowd, a few familiar faces stand out. Marco and Roxy were set up in the middle of the clearing, jamming to Disturbed's "Down with the Sickness."

My gaze stops when I notice Jay a few yards away from where we were heading. He was leaning against a neon green Aston Martin racing car. I wonder briefly if it's his or if he knows the driver. My eyes take in everything about him from the Nikes on his feet, traveling up to his faded jeans that hang from his hips, and that thin line of tan skin barely visible from the edge of the dark blue Henley shirt. His red baseball hat was flipped backward. He looked amazing. My heart thudded to a halt when the same blonde from the party the other night slings her arm around his waist. I watch him pull her closer, his hand falling down to rest against her ass, which was barely covered in a black leather skirt. She looks beautiful and very cold. For some reason, tears pricked at the corners of my eyes causing my nose to sting.

As if he can feel my gaze on him, Jay's head shoots up. I look away just in time and plaster a fake smile on my lips while I follow Toni over to where the guys were standing in a circle.

"Blaise!" Joey yells, pulling me into a side hug. His other arm is wrapped around a pretty Native American girl I don't recognize. I'd kill for her thick hair though. We both smiled and laughed at Joey's attempt to hug us together.

"'Sup, little B?" Stone's voice cuts across the circle. I lift my chin at him in response. The party continues around me, and I let myself sink into the familiarity of it. The bass pounds causing vibrations in my chest. The smell of the open air, the roar of the engines in the distance and the cheer from the crowd; I miss nights like this.

Stone watches me from where he was standing with a knowing look on his face. Blake... he had loved nights at Scar, too. He lived for them. Without thinking, I make my way over until I am standing right in front of Stone. He hands me a beer, towering over me in the process. I take it from him, twisting the cap off easily. Four months sober and now I've drunk two weekends in a row. Party on, Blaise.

"Ya thinking about him, too?" Stone asks me.

"Always," I respond. He nods, biting his lower lip. Stone was hot, there was no doubt about it. He is a few years older than me, but like his name, Stone was all beautifully angled and hard. He rarely smiles. His demeanor icy. Stone wasn't nice to me, but he wasn't mean either. He has always just been distant. He watches and doesn't speak unless he has something to say.

"I miss him," he tells me before his eyes sweep the crowd, hiding any emotion from me. I just nodded in response.

"Hey, guys!" Toni waves us toward the tracks. "Joe is up next!" I notice that the majority of the crowd was now moving toward the lined up cars. My gaze swings to Joey's car only to find Jay leaning against the side as well. He looks down at the engine with Bobby, a kid I graduated with, who works at the garage in town. The blonde was still attached to his hip, practically embedding her fake claws into his forearm. I look away before he catches me staring again. I'm angry at myself for thinking about him as much as I have been when he clearly doesn't care. Obviously the other night was an anomaly enhanced by liquid courage.

I make myself focus on Joey who was buckling himself in before the crowd pushes off to the sides. Joey and Bobby pull their cars toward the front line. I can feel the weight from Jay's gaze on me now that he has seen me. Feeling embarrassed, I shrink further into Stone and Toni who are standing on both sides, flanking me. I try distracting my brain watching Joey whip around the outside edges, cutting Bobby off in the third corner, giving him the momentum he needs to race across the finish line. I cheer with everyone else around me when he comes to a stop. Seeing Joey race was almost poetical. He could handle any car or motorcycle and drive flawlessly. He lacked fear which was dangerous for any opponent in a race. Watching Joey at Scar again had my heart racing.

Joey drives his car back over to where we were standing, sliding out of his seat, and collecting money from anyone who had made the poor choice to bet against him. Bobby drives back to where his friends are, only this time when I glance, Jay and the blonde are gone. They left together. My heart pinches. I push down the emotion, close it off, and sweep the pain away. I have no claim on Jay.

"Blaise," Toni says, laughing at me, he must have said my name a couple of times judging by everyone else's expressions.

"Sorry," I tell him, my cheeks blushing.

"It's okay." He laughs again. "We're going to Marco's, a few people are heading there, want to go?"

It's a tempting offer, but the thought of my bed suddenly seemed much better. I wasn't sure if it was because Jay showed up with another girl or the memories from being at Scar, but I'm suddenly just ready to be by myself again.

"Nah," I respond, shaking my head. "It's been fun, but I should get back. Got to work in the AM. I'll catch a ride with that chick I work with," I tell them, nodding over at Molly.

They all nod, giving me side hugs before disappearing into the crowd. I wait before heading into the darkness toward the trail leading to the main road. I lied about getting a ride from Molly, deciding a run back into town would be better for me. The farther away from the fire and crowd I get, the colder I began to feel. I wrap my arms around my frame, walking fast, suddenly aware that someone was following behind me. I whip around, almost tripping over my feet before slamming into Jay's solid body.

"What are you doing?" he asks, stepping toward me as I continue backing up.

"What are you talking about?" I ask, cocking my head to the side.

"You shouldn't be here," he spits venomously, his jaw clenching.

"I was invited," I throw over my shoulder as I turn back around, sprinting toward a vacant car in the distance. I could give two fucks about what Jay has to say right now. He spent all night ignoring me with some chick all over him and now he's demanding to know why I'm here. He has no claim on me.

"It's dangerous," I hear him say, his voice a whisper of breath against the sensitive skin on the back of my neck.

"You're here," I remind him, whipping back around ready for a confrontation. I suck in my breath when his chest pushes against my front. His head tilts down so he can look into my eyes. Those dark brown orbs probe mine, reading my thoughts and analyzing my secrets. He makes my knees weak. I chew on my bottom lip anxiously, waiting for him to speak, when his eyes dart down following the movements of my teeth.

"I'm working," he replies, though he looks distracted.

I laugh. "Is that what you call it?" I scoff before practically sprinting the short distance to the road. He chuckles behind me.

"Are you jealous, Blaise?" I stopped dead in my tracks, my fists clenching until my short nails leave crescent moons in my palm.

I turn around ready to flip him off, instead Jay grabs my arms, spinning me until my back hits the side of the abandoned car. He crowds closer while I'm still in shock. My back rests against the tinted window, his torso holding me in place. Our hands grapple, fighting for dominance. I try to push away, but he slams me back again. I release one hand and bring it up, resting it on his chest, pushing against him to give myself space.

"Come here," he breathes against my lips before taking my mouth with his. He tastes so good, minty with a hint of liquor. My lips answer every pull and sweep of his tongue, my body melts into his, and my legs climb up around his waist to grip him tighter against me. His hands release my wrists and I automatically entwine my arms around his neck. I can feel the brutal force of his grip on my backside.

Everything around us blurs and disappears until it's just him and I. His body demands more, rocking into me, forcing my legs to tighten farther around his waist until the inside of my thighs shake. It was like he had a hot wire to my brain when he starts rolling his hips slower and pressing harder. My breath hitches and lodges in my throat when I feel him slide his hand between our bodies. Strong fingers grab through the material of my jeans adding pressure right where I crave it. Three more controlled strokes and I'm coming undone, my body buckles and sags into him. A small moan escapes from my lips.

Jay sets me down suddenly, my feet barely touch the ground before he's pulling himself away from me.

"Fuck," he mutters under his breath. My cheeks heat red, and suddenly I feel embarrassed. I march away from the car as fast as

I can on shaky legs, ready to put this night behind me and sleep off the feeling of being unwanted. Jay's warm hand wraps around mine, pulling me to a stop before he's back in my space. His hands cradle my face, forcing my eyes up. I know tears are shimmering in mine, and I prepare myself to see the pity or rejection in his. My breath catches. His dark orbs eat mine hungrily. Soft lips touch my forehead causing me to shiver slightly.

"Get in the car, baby. I'll take you home." His words mean something in my brain, only my body can't respond. I think I'm in shock. Jay once again has managed to turn my world upside down.

Confused and turned on, my body still humming from the explosiveness, I get in the car as Jay rounds to the other side and gets in too.

"This is your car?" I ask, my brain and mouth starting to connect again. His eyes slide to mine and he smirks.

"Didn't think I'd dry fuck you against just anyone's car, did you?" he responds. I don't answer because honestly, I hadn't been thinking at all. A total random person could have been inside the car and I wouldn't have noticed.

"Where's your truck?" I say while still trying to process my life.

"I returned it," he answers while carefully maneuvering over the bumpy path to the main road. He cracks the windows and lets the breeze in.

"I thought it was yours," I respond with a shrug of my shoulder.

"I don't like having the same vehicle for more than a few days when I'm on certain cases." His voice drops off as if he said more than he wanted. My heart thuds in my chest and fear coils down my spine. Being near Jay makes me forget the why of him being here. Murder. He hits the play button on his radio and the Red Hot Chili Peppers floods the small space. I relax back into my seat while he drives us back toward civilization.

When we get to my apartment complex, Jay parks the car with ease into my mom's empty spot before shutting off the ignition. He moves as if he's done this a hundred times before. Like it's a memory ingrained in his mind and he doesn't ask for my direction. My mouth parts in surprise, the questions are on the tip of my tongue, but Jay moves faster. Before I can blink, he opens my door, dragging me from the car, and pulls my body against his again. Any alarm bells that were about to go off are now on silent. His hands run from my shoulders down to my waist leaving scorching heat in their wake. One touch and I realize I don't have it in me to lie about where my mom is. Lie that he shouldn't come in because we wouldn't be alone, or to even pretend that I'm not basically on my own, living with my brother's ghost. Not tonight, tonight I want to feel like I did the last time Jay touched me, even if he doesn't remember. Jay's been bringing life into me again, just by being in this town and he doesn't even know it.

Jay's mouth was on mine. His hands pull me closer and I cling to him, pulling him into me. I ignore how right and how perfect this feels. Without separating, we manage to get to my apartment. Somehow we get in the door while he lifts me off my feet, half carrying and half dragging my body down the narrow hallway right into my room.

The street light across the road sheds an orange glow through the room contrasting with the darkness. I can sense Jay's eyes on me, watching me. I feel sexy and bold, my fingers slowly lifting the hem of my tank top, exposing skin to him. The fire in his eyes encourages me to keep going. I quickly throw the top off over my head. My hands go down to my pants, undoing the button and peeling them off my legs. Standing in front of him in my lace boy shorts and bra is not awkward, but familiar. His eyes rake my body up and down.

Wanting to entice him further, my fingers skate to the back of my bra to the clasp.

"Don't," Jay says, his voice husky. He moves toward me slowly, like a predator and I'm the chosen prey. His hand snakes out, wrapping around mine, and pulling my hands away from the clasp. His eyes, now hooded, never leaving mine. He lifts the hat from his head and sets it down on my dresser. It fits perfectly in the empty spot as if it was meant to be there. His shirt lands next to mine on the floor. For the first time I get to look at his perfectly sculpted chest. Lean muscles twitch on his six-pack under my gaze. Jay is all smooth, tan skin except for a trail of dark hair around his navel that descends into his jeans. A single tattoo is etched across his left pec. A cross with two sets of Roman numeral writing weaves around it.

"Like what you see?" Jay asks, a hint of a smile on his lips. I was totally checking him out and I didn't care. I reach my hand out letting my fingers run over each groove and dip, feeling the heat emanating off him. His breath hitches and a flush sits high on his cheekbones. My body shakes when he groans, and I slip my fingers under the waistband of his briefs. Last time I didn't get to feel or take the time to explore Jay. We had been frantic and the timing was urgent. This time we could stay in the moment. I could enjoy every inch of Jay. My hand wraps around the silky smooth skin of his cock, rubbing up and down until his head falls back in surrender.

"Blaise." My name is scratchy coming from his mouth before his hand wraps around my wrist, yanking my hand away from him. I don't get a chance to protest before he's all over me, my panties drop, my bra falls to the floor, and my body is pushed down onto my bed. A slight chill ripples over my skin when he detaches from me long enough to slip his pants down and free himself. I watch fascinated as he rolls the condom down his length before climbing over me.

Without warning, Jay pushes his body into mine, impaling my hips to the bed. I hiss at the fullness, a silent cry leaving my mouth before a wave of tingles flush my body. Our eyes meet, his brown orbs are pitch black, one of his hands cups my neck, pulling me into a primal kiss. His lips are strong as they guide mine, pulling, biting, and messy to the point our teeth clash a few times. I struggle to breathe, the loss of oxygen only intensifying my building orgasm. Each thrust from Jay pushes my body up the bed. I wrap one arm around his neck and use the other to push back against the wall before my head slams into it.

"Jay," I moan into his mouth. I'm nearing the edge, every slam of his hips hitting my clit at just the right angle with the perfect amount of pressure. Sweat beads form on my temples, and my fingers clutch at the skin on his shoulders. Everything in my body is wound tight.

"Let go, baby," he practically growls into my mouth, and I do. I come all over his cock. Jay pulls back, his eyes dilating as he watches me experience my orgasm. His body rides mine out before his hips jerk sharply and a low groan escapes him.

I finally breathe, taking in long pulls of air, yet I still can't make myself let him go. Thankfully, he seems just as reluctant to let me go. His body pins mine to the bed, except for his forearms that he's braced on, bracketing around my head. He catches his breath before me and dips his lips to mine, gently this time. My lips and chin are raw and swollen from the scrape of his facial hair.

"I'm going to stay," he says with authority. I can only nod my head in response, still completely shaken from the sex with this man. He rolls onto his back, taking me with him and tucking my body into his side. He moves to the edge of the bed, grabs his cell phone from the floor and places it on my nightstand. The light from the screen casts an eerie glow. The light reflects on the silver chamber of a Colt 1911 45ACP. My body tenses. That is not the usual 9mm Glock that is law enforcement issued. The handgun that Sarge and the other guys in blue wear around town.

"Go to sleep," Jay says, gripping my chin and pulling my gaze back to him. "Everything is alright. I got it." The sincere mask that drops over his face melts my chills. Of course, he knows what he's doing.

I licked my lips. "Okay," I whisper, accepting his protection, allowing a piece of myself to give up control and trust him.

"Goodnight, babe," he murmurs, kissing my forehead.

"'Night, Jay," I answer before burrowing my face against his shoulder. My room has lost its glow, the light across the street finally going out, yet I don't feel scared. There is no sense of loneliness sitting on my chest. My thoughts are peaceful, and my breathing evens out until everything shuts off and I sleep.

Eight

I PINCH MY EYES TOGETHER, ignoring the sunlight streaming in from my window, letting out a huff of frustration. Jay opened my curtain again. Sure enough, I hear the shower turn off in the bathroom across the hall. My mom is down south for work for a few days and I know it isn't her. I keep waiting for Jay to say something about her and her lack of existence in my home, but he doesn't. He's probably just glad she hasn't been around all week to hear him nail her daughter every night. Every night this week, Jay has been in my bed. Usually after driving me home from work, something he insists on doing. Just as he insists on hanging out at the bar most nights a few hours left into my shift. Luis has started to notice. Thank fuck he hasn't said anything. All I got was a lift of his eyebrow and small grunt. Jay pays his tab every night and leaves a generous tip, so Luis can't complain too much.

"You're awake," Jay says, walking back into my room. I roll onto my back and watch him cross the room to the small stack of clean clothes he placed there last night. My blue towel sits low on his hips. A few water droplets slide down his chest. I can't form coherent thoughts except that I wish I was those water beads right now. My tongue darts out to my lips.

"Stop that," Jay announces before turning and giving me his back.

"That's not helping," I tell him, groaning. When did my hormones become those of a thirteen-year-old boy? I want Jay all the time. His body on mine, next to mine, inside mine. His laugh gives me tingles, his voice makes my knees shake, and his touch warms everything inside mine. It's been a week of playing house and he's embedded his way into my life. He feeds an addiction I wasn't aware that I had. I've never felt this way about anyone else before and it should scare the ever-living crap out of me.

"What time do you start today?" he asks, a hint of a smile tugs at his lips like he knows that he's twisting me up in knots.

"Lunch shift today," I tell him. "Twelve to five, then I told Sarge I'd eat dinner at the ranch tonight."

He turns and frowns. "Did I know about that?"

I sit up, hugging my knees to my chest and shrug. "Probably not," I tell him. "We made the plans over a week ago."

"Oh," he answers, dropping the towel to slide his briefs and jeans on. "So, I don't get to see you tonight?"

I shake my head no, watching in fascination as his face darkens. His jaw clenches and the muscles in his forearms ripple when his fists tighten. "You could come over after?" I ask, hesitation coating my voice. I feel like it's the wrong answer on a test I'm taking.

"Yeah," he says, pulling his black t-shirt over his head. He doesn't say anything else, averting his eyes while he pockets his cell phone and wallet from my nightstand. He tucks the Colt in the back of his waistband before he brings his gaze back to mine. Disappointment ripples through my chest when I see the blank mask over his face. "I'll call you then," he tells me. I swallow down the lump in my throat, hoping I won't cry. I hate feeling insecure like I did something wrong.

"Are you mad?" I ask timidly, hating to be one of those girls, not sure how ready he is to share feelings. He blinks before dragging his hand over the top of his hair.

"Is that Blake's room down the hall?" he asks. I pause, not thinking I heard him right. Judging by the stiffness of his body posture, I'm assuming we are not going to talk about our feelings.

Instead, I nod my head. "Yeah," I say, clearing my throat. "My mom won't pack it up. It's exactly as he left it when we moved out." I keep my eyes down on the comforter, letting him see my insides. "I haven't been in there since the funeral either. I tried once to box some stuff up, but she got mad."

"People deal with grief in different ways," he says, his voice softer than it was a few minutes ago. I shrug in response. Tears tickle the edges of my eyes.

"I just feel like he'd want us to let go, ya know? Like his things are holding him here or something. He haunts the room." I share my secret lightly.

"You haven't been in there since the funeral?" he asks quietly.

"No," I tell him again. "She closed the door and it's just stayed that way." I don't tell him how scared I am to open the door and face all the memories waiting there. I wish she'd pack it away. I wish I had the courage to do it. It's one of those things that parents should have to do. I'm the kid, it shouldn't be me. Cleaning out the place we lived in for a year was bad enough. His high school room, our childhood room would be worse.

"Where did you put everything from your guys' apartment?" he asks, watching me closely. My cheeks heat when I realize I spoke out loud.

"I threw away what I couldn't take with me in the car. The rest of the boxes are in a storage shed for now," I answer.

He nods. "Whenever you are ready to say goodbye, I'll help you. We can do it when your mom isn't around. But if it makes you feel better, I'll be here."

My chest warms at his words. "Thanks," I mumble, unable to look at him.

He pushes off my dresser and crosses the room, hovering over me. "Drive safe," he says before pecking my lips lightly. I'm stunned and emotionally drained from our conversation. My eyes close against the burn from the tears, my heart thundering in my chest.

"The hell," I whisper to myself. I listen to the main door close and hear the rumble of his engine before I drag myself down the hall to twist the locks in place again.

I quickly decide that my morning is already off to a shitty start and can foresee the whole day going this way. I pick up my cell and scroll through the numbers, mentally psyching myself up to take the needed day to myself. My thumb hovers over Luis' name while I catalog all the bills that still need to get paidthis month. I exhale a slow breath and let go of any thoughts to play hooky today. Frustrated, I grab my towel off the chair and head for the shower. If I'm not going to call in sick, I may as well go in early.

An hour later, my black hair is stick straight and pulled into a high ponytail on the top of my head. My Aerosmith t-shirt dress lightly grazes the black thigh-high boots on my feet, and it's causing heads to turn. I'm oblivious to it although, as usual, because behind the bar I can zone out. Turning to the cash register,

I pause when I hear Luis' rumbling, "Here we go."

I whipped my head around and watch as Joey, Stone, and Antonio walked through the door and head to their favorite booth in the back. My chest squeezes with familiarity. I've seen this sight so many times before. My breath catches, waiting for Blake and Seth to join them. The minute the thought slips through my mind, it's like a cold bucket of water being splashed on me.

"Can you believe that?" Jenna questions right next to me and I jump in surprise.

"What?" I ask, trying to think if she said anything else while my mind was in the past.

"That," Jenna says, pointing to where the guys are sitting. Molly is reaching over to grab the menu from the table, giving the guys a front row seat to her awesome rack. "Can she put it out there anymore?"

I laugh. "I mean, she is a waitress. Sometimes for tips, you do what a girl's gotta do. Plus they're hot," I tell her. Jenna's face instantly reddens and her eyes narrow.

"They're not that hot." She points her finger at me accusingly.

"I thought you were over him," I remind her, swatting her hand out of my face.

"I am," Jenna answers quickly. "It's just, you know that girl thing, I'm over him, but I want him to know he missed out on a great thing." She shrugs her shoulders.

"You're joking," I say, questioningly.

She rolls her eyes. "You can't tell me, Blaise, that if Seth were here right now, you'd love nothing more than for your new hottie boyfriend to walk in the door and rub his face in it."

"Okay." I hold up my finger. "One, you're a little vindictive, and two Seth and I dated for a hot second in high school. We were always way better friends than anything else, and three... Jay is not my boyfriend."

She nods her head, grinning. "Sure. Did you tell him that?"

"What are you talking about?" I ask her, pulling a blank look over my face.

Jenna tips her head to the side, her hands slide to her waist. "He's here all the time to see you and I know you leave with him at night sometimes."

"Stalker?" I ask, raising my eyebrow at her. I didn't realize how many people were paying attention to what Jay and I were doing. He told me to act like we knew each other, but I wasn't sure if he wanted to give off the vibe that we were dating. I felt on alert, the defensive side of myself pushing to the front.

"Whatever, babe," Jenna says, smirking before walking away to bring her table their drink order. I watch her go, swallowing past the cotton dryness in my mouth. Her words were eating at me and I didn't know why.

"Hey, Blaise," Molly called next to me. "Can you run these beers to the guys? They wanted to talk to you," she explains to me, lifting her shoulders before walking to the kitchen.

"Ah." My eyes shoot to their booth and sure enough they're all looking at me, too. "Sure."

"I'll watch the bar," Jenna says, she's next to me again leaning over to put her tray away.

I make my way over to them, fighting to keep my face neutral. We haven't talked since the night at Scar. I wasn't avoiding them, there just never seemed to be an opportunity to see them.

"Hey guys," I say while placing the three Coronas in front of them. Some things never do change.

"Hi, B," Joey responds, giving me a smile that doesn't quite reach his eyes.

"How've you been?" I ask, forcing small talk and trying to act normal.

"Busy," Stone replies for them. I nod and smile.

"How about you?" Toni asks, lifting an eyebrow. I don't miss the way his brown eyes slide over me from head to toe.

"Busy," I answer, shrugging my shoulders. "The usual." A look passed between the three of them.

"Heard you know the new guy over at Rowley's." A smirk tugs at his lips. I feel my cheeks turning pink knowing they are referring to Jay.

"Jarrod Knight or something?" Stone throws in. Confusion slides over my face before I can mask it. He's watching me closely.

"I just know him as Jay." I clear my throat, trying to appear not affected. "I don't really know him that well."

"Right," Joey responds, laughing. I frown. "Oh come on, Blaise. Everyone has seen you together. He's here almost every day to see you."

"We're just hanging out," I answered noncommittally, my mind still firing rapidly that Stone called Jay, Jarrod.

"Okay." Toni laughs.

"Look," I tell them, slinging my tray under my arm. "I don't know what else to tell you. If all you called me over here for was to give me a hard time, fine, congrats. Can I go back to work now?" My eyes slide over each of them. Anger had seeped into my words on its own and I could tell they were bothered by it. Toni and Joey's gazes fell to the table. When my gaze clashed with Stone's, a smile tugged at the edges of his mouth.

"Sorry, little B." He shrugs. "We didn't want to make you mad. If Blake were here, I think he'd be asking the same questions."

"He would have already been over to the garage and questioning him about his intentions," Joey pipes in, grinning.

"We just felt like we should watch over you in his place, Blaisey."

Toni's voice cracks when he speaks. "Seems like he's into you and we just wanted to feel you out about him."

Guilt slams into my chest.

"I don't really know him," I say, my voice thick with emotion. "I know he works part-time at Rowley's and part-time at Sarge's helping on the ranch."

"K," Stone replies. His fingers graze over his chin. I keep my eyes averted, hoping he can't read the bullshit in mine. "When is your shift over?"

"At five," I answer.

"We're heading to Marco's tonight. Want to go with us?" Joey asks.

I bite my lip. "I'm supposed to have dinner with Sarge and the family tonight."

"Oh, okay." Joey shrugs before taking a drink from his glass.

"Next time," I tell them before giving it another thought. They all nod in agreement, which causes my chest to tighten in pain. I've heard them out about why they've been absent from my life for the past few months. I need to just accept it and get over it. A small part of me though treads back and forth feeling uneasy. The same part of me also warning me to be cautious with Jay or Jarrod, whatever the hell his name is. "I have to get back behind the bar. Next beer is on me, so let Molly know, okay?" I tell them, trying a genuine smile.

"Will do, Blaise." Stone nods his head. I walk briskly back to the bar, giving Luis an apologetic smile before making up the next drink ticket. My mind shuffles around my conversation with the guys. I don't know if I'm more pissed or touched that they are asking about my supposed relationship with Jay. I can't help feeling leery about Jay using a different name, and why he wouldn't tell me about it? The more I'm around him I feel like I'm being set up for failure. There are too many questions and not nearly enough explanations.

My shift flies by, my mind and my body both checked out on different tasks. The guys eventually leave, yet the uneasiness in my gut stays. When the clock reads four fifty-nine, I hand the cash register key over to my replacement and hand my receipts over to Luis.

"Be right back," he mumbles, heading back to his office to get the cash from my tips.

"Ready to go?" a deep voice with an east coast accent asks right next to my ear, causing goosebumps to slide over my arms. My head whips around to face Jay, and I let my blank mask fall into place.

"Jarrod, right?" I tease, lifting my brow and dragging my gaze over him. I don't miss the way his posture tightens and his jaw clenches before a shit-eating grin pulls his lips apart.

"Let's go, baby." He drapes his arm across my shoulders. "Tomas, Pricilla, and the kids are waiting."

"Luis is grabbing my cash," I tell him, trying to shrug his arm off. To my displeasure, this causes him to hold on to me tighter. Jay jogs away to the back office. Before I have the chance to blink again, he's handing me a stack of cash.

"Let's go." He grabs my wrist, pulling me behind him out through the sea of bodies toward the door. The minute the dry heat hits my face, I wrench my arm out of his grip.

"What are you doing here?" I demand, my chest rising and falling while I attempt to keep my cool.

Not fazed by my anger, Jay opens up the car door for me. "Get in and I'll explain on the way."

We standoff outside the car, neither of us willing to give in. My gaze holds his and I can see his cool demeanor starting to slip.

"Get the fuck in, Blaise," he tells me between clenched teeth.

Smirking, I move in closer until my lips are a breath away from his. To any onlookers, it would look like I'm going in for a kiss. Instead, I went in for the kill.

"I'll get in when I feel like it. And when I do, you will answer my questions or else I'm done helping you get any information. Okay, Jarrod?" I make sure my voice is as sweet as honey. His eyes meet mine and I'm not prepared for the emotional storm brewing in those dark depths. A flush creeps up his cheekbones and if he clenched his teeth any harder, I was sure that vein in the middle of his forehead would burst. He nods and I slip past him before sinking into the seat. My door slams shut next to me. My body shakes with the tension I'm holding onto. Every small step forward with him feels like twenty steps back. Jay folds himself into the car next to me and starts the engine. We don't talk until the tires hit the asphalt road heading toward the Ramirez ranch.

"Spill," I grit out, turning my body to face his. He glances at me before looking back at the road.

"You really have so little faith in me?" he asks.

I shrug. "I don't really know you, Jarrod. I know you work for law enforcement and you're supposedly investigating my brother's death. But you lied about your name, so who knows what else you're lying about."

"I'm not fucking lying about my name. My name is Jay McCall. Don't believe me, here's my phone. Call my mom and ask her. She's a sweet little lady who lives in the Boston area in the same house I grew up in. I'm undercover on an important case involving one of my closest friends, your brother, so no, I'm not going to go around introducing myself with my real name to every possible criminal in the city." He spews the words venomously, his cell phone chucked into my lap.

"What are you doing here?" I ask again. "You knew I had plans tonight."

"You said you were going to Ramirez's. I wanted to spend time with you," he answers, his knuckles turning white as he grips the steering wheel.

"I asked you to see me after and you got all weird about it," I remind him.

He shrugs. "Why is it so bad that I want to be with you? I don't care if it's at Señor Locos, your house, or the Ramirez's."

"Why?" I wanted to know. "I think there's more to this whole thing than you're being honest about. People already think we're dating so you being around all the time is already explainable."

He scoffs. "I don't care what other people think. I'm working and I know what I have to do to close this case. I wasn't planning on this though." He sighs, sounding frustrated.

"I don't need you sticking to me," I tell him. My voice sounding stronger than I feel right now.

"Blaise," Jay says my name while pinching the bridge of his nose with his fingers. "I like you, okay? This thing with us… has nothing to do with the case right now."

I'm speechless and he stops talking the last few miles before we hit the gravel road to the house. My cheeks flame and my heart is rioting around in my chest. I swallow past the lump that formed in my throat. Before I can completely compose myself, he stops the car in front of the house. We sit in silence before he grabs my hand from my lap. "I meant what I just said." His jaw clenches and he holds my gaze hostage. "I have to lie to everyone else right now, and I'm fine with that if it means getting the information I need. I am Jarrod Knight to them. You get the truth. Even if you mess up and call me Jay accidentally, it sounds like a nickname for Jarrod."

"Sounds like you put a lot of thought into it," I say, pulling my hand away.

His hand shoots out, gripping my chin between his thumb and index finger, holding me in place. "I had to. It's my job. If I don't think twenty steps ahead, I could die."

Jay watches me intently, his gaze jumping all over my face trying to read me. I can't stop the pang of guilt in my chest. I know I overreacted. Logically, I know he probably has more he can't tell me and I'm not sure I would want to know even if he could. Tears sting my eyes and I fight to keep them at bay. There are too many emotions battling between us. Our past hangs above my head while the present seems like a game of Lava. One wrong step and you're doomed.

"How old are you, Jay?" My voice breaks, betraying me.

"Twenty-seven," he answers without hesitation.

"Does that bother you?" I ask. Our age gap looms like an ever-present complication.

"I think I should be the one asking you that." He smirks. "I don't care about your age, Blaise. You may only be eighteen, but you've experienced more than most people will in their lifetime. You've had to grow up when you should have been a kid. You have crazy good work ethic and you care about everyone, even to those who don't deserve it."

I snort. "I wouldn't go that far."

He quirks his eyebrow. "Blaise, if you didn't care, it wouldn't bother you so much that your mom is never home."

"How—"

"Work hazards. I notice more than is necessary sometimes." He shrugs like it's not a big deal, but it is. My head hangs down, trying to hide my embarrassment. Of course, she's never home. She's never been the parent we needed. Instead of holding us closer, she pushed us away when our dad left. I remember her screaming at Blake when we were little and had our first visit from CPS. She blamed everything on him, including our dad leaving.

"Hey," he whispers, his hands now hold my face and I'm forced to look at him again, "None of that is your fault. It wasn't Blake's either. You guys got dealt a shitty hand with parents. And it's normal to still care because she is your mom. You're grieving… for Blake and for her."

"We should go inside," I say, breaking the silence. I've had enough of the emotions talk. A sad smile tugs at Jay's mouth, but he nods anyway. I launch myself out of his car, practically sprinting to the front door. Before I can knock, the heavy slab of wood swings open.

"'Bout time," Sarge says sarcastically. "I was about ready to shine my flashlight on you out there, but Pricilla told me to give you time."

"Sorry, Sarge," I tell him, feeling the blush stain my cheeks.

"My fault," Jay says, walking in right behind me. His hand lingers on my back and I know Sarge can see the gesture. "I was begging for forgiveness in advance before I leave tomorrow."

"Heading back already?" Sa asks. They continue on with their conversation, oblivious that I've gone completely still. My head hurts from all the surprise bombs being dropped tonight. I can't wait to get back in the car again.

Dinner passes by agonizingly slow. If it wasn't for Pricilla's enchiladas, and Nico and Katy's stories, the whole night would have been pure torture. Jay must sense my restlessness because he has kept a grip on my knee all night. This time I'm ready before Jay even turns the keys in the ignition.

"Why didn't you tell me you're leaving?"

"I just found out this morning. That's why I was mad you had plans tonight. I took off from the garage early to go to dinner with you."

"Are you coming back?" The one question that has been plaguing me since dinner.

"What?" His head whips to look at me before back at the road, "Yes. I'm just going to chase a lead. I'll be back Monday or Tuesday, depending on what I find."

"Oh," I say, my shoulders sagging in relief. "Can you tell me about it?"

"No," he answers while grabbing my hand with his. "Not yet. When I'm absolutely sure, I'll share, but right now I can't. Please trust me, Blaise." I squeeze his hand in response. I hate being left in the dark. I want to know his secrets.

We're quiet the rest of the way back to my place, just the sounds of Red's "Coming Apart" floating in the space around us. Jay parks in the empty spot and I realize I don't have to worry about it anymore. Not even for appearances sake and I suddenly feel the exhaustion.

"Are you coming in?" I ask, hating how my voice sounds and praying he doesn't think I'm clingy now.

"I wish I could." His fingers reach out and pushes a strand of my hair behind my ear, the slight touch causes chills across my neck. "I have to head out now to get to the air space in time."

"Air space, huh?" I try laughing to ease the sadness.

"Yeah," he responds before stepping closer. My breath sucks in when his hands wrap around my back, pulling my body against his. "Be safe, okay?" he asks, attempting to smile.

"I think that's my line," I tell him before laying my cheek against his chest. I hear the strong beat of his heart through his thin grey t-shirt. He laughs and the sound vibrates through his whole chest.

"I'll be fine," he tells me before laying his head on top of mine. Time slides by while we stand there holding each other. I've never felt so comfortable being held by someone, but in Jay's arms, everything was peaceful again.

"I'll call you when I can," he tells me before leaning down to touch his lips to mine. I nod, causing our mouths to brush.

"Okay," I breathe out and inhale him in again. "I'll miss you."

His body stills for a moment before a smile touches his lips. When his body detangles from mine, I feel cold. Jay waits for me to get up to my door and get inside. Before the last deadbolt slides into place, I hear his engine rev to life then fades away.

The apartment is dark, except for the overhead light in the kitchen. From memory, I make my way to my room and drop to my bed. The silence is thick in the room. I'm alone again. A ping from my phone causes me to jump in surprise. I smile, wondering if Jay is regretting that he didn't stay now. I swipe my passcode and bring my messages up. Three words and my heart plunges into my stomach. My hand shakes while I slide my legs up to my chest, wrapping my arms around myself.

Unknown: DON'T TRUST ANYONE

Nine

SEVENTY-TWO HOURS PASSED since I received that ominous text. Seventy-two hours where I did not sleep, watched my back, and kept my head down. Seventy-two hours where I tried relentlessly to text the person back only to receive a message that my messages failed to send. Every call and message to Jay went unanswered. I would have thought he'd be jumping at the bit to hear about this, but he ghosted. I even dug so low as to attempt calling Antonio, Stone and Joey only to find out they were working in Vegas and weren't around either. Chills zipped down my spine when I realized they were all gone at the same time and whoever sent that text had to have known this.

Jay said he'd be back Monday, Tuesday at the latest, and it was now Thursday night. My nerves were strung tight. My eyes were bloodshot from my lack of sleep and I still had to get through my next shift at Locos. I was agitated and my old friend isolation had settled back into my heart. I was alone, like always, only now someone was watching me. Today should have been my day off, instead I picked up a dinner shift for a server whose baby got sick and she didn't have daycare. My body was running purely on autopilot.

I heard him before I saw him, Joey's laugh would make anyone stop and look. I freeze as all three of them and Sarge came filing in through the door. My mind spins while my jaw drops open in shock. I have to be hallucinating.

"B!" Toni yells before hitting his hands against the bar. "Just the person we're looking for."

I pull back, blinking a few times to make sure I'm seeing things clearly. When my eyes clear Stone, Toni, Joey, and Sarge are all watching me. Smiles on the other three's faces while Sarge looks a little apprehensive.

"Why are you looking for me?" I ask as I turn to face Toni, trying to keep my posture relaxed.

"We're going to Scar tonight, want to come with us?" Toni asks, his face lighting up.

"Thought we could talk about that text you sent us," Stone adds, shrugging. My heart lurches.

"Maybe?" I turn back to Toni, answering. "Depends on how busy we get tonight."

"Sounds good, Blaisey," Joey says, tapping on the bar.

"What can I help you with Sarge?" I ask him, trying to find a smile.

"Just a water for me, Blaise. I'm just waiting on Jarrod. I need to bring the receipts in from the hay haul I sent him on."

I still again, before nodding. I'm probably supposed to know this was their cover story. All the lies being told are starting to add up. I glance at the guys through my lashes, but they're not paying any attention to me.

"I forgot he got back today," I reply, the words feel like sawdust in my mouth. I didn't know shit and I wonder if Sarge knew that.

"He got back last night," he replies, and I catch him wincing. My hand freezes with the ice scoop halfway in the bucket. While I was panicking by myself all night, Jay had been back in town. I grit my jaw before handing the glass of water to Sarge.

"Probably didn't want to wake me," I respond, playing my part and playing along.

"We'll take that table over there," Sarge says, backing away to the closest booth. I nod again before placing a tray of mugs into the washer. My insides are screaming.

"When did you get back?" I ask Stone, passing their beers to them.

"About an hour ago," he responds, handing the beers out. "Stopped here first to eat, then we'll get cleaned up and catch a few z's until we need to leave."

"Eleven again?" I ask him and he nods. I'm about to respond when his eyes slide past me and fixate on the door. I don't have to look to know what caught his attention. The hairs on my exposed neck rise and burning awareness slide through my veins. I hate his effect on me right now. My cheeks flush with anger.

"Catch you later?" Stone asks me, and I nod.

"I'll be there," I confirm now that I've made up my mind. Like hell am I going to sit around and wait for Jay to decide when he can be in my life, and when he can't.

"Hey." Jay's voice carries from where he's now standing by the bar. My gaze flings to his, taking in his appearance. He looks freshly showered and flawless as if he had a great night of sleep. Meanwhile, I look like the doped up version of Cruella De Ville.

"What can I get you?" I ask him, my lips forming a smile and the sweet little server voice rolls off my tongue. I'm determined not to give Jay any of my time.

His jaw clenches. "Can I talk to you?"

I tilt my head to the side. "I'm working right now."

"After work?" he tries again.

"I have plans," I tell him, shrugging my shoulders. "Better put your order in, Sarge said he's waiting for you," I tell him, nodding to the booth. Jay's eyes never leave me. Blood races through me knowing I'm the main focus of his attention.

"I'm not going anywhere," he says quiet enough that only my ears catch it. "I need to talk to you."

Not fazed by his caveman act, I shrug my shoulders again. "I'm busy," I repeat, holding up the new drink ticket in front of me. He nods, his hand sliding into his pockets.

"I'll come back later," he tells me before heading over to the booth with Sarge.

"We'll see," I mumble to myself. He might be back later, but I have no intentions of being here when he does.

The next few hours are fast-paced and I'm flying high on adrenaline. My senses kick up when the guys leave, calling out that they'll see me later, and they left a generous tip. I'm aware that Sarge and Jay heard them leave. Jay's gaze practically burns holes in my back as I continue shuffling around the bar. Not long after, Sarge and Jay get up to leave. I'm not surprised as they both head toward me.

"You doing okay?" Sarge asks, and I feel his concern. I'm sure by now Jay has told him that I blew up his phone while he was gone.

I shrug. "It is, what it is," I tell him. I feel bad holding back on Sarge. I know he's helping Jay and probably has his heart in the right place. I should have called him, but I didn't. I never want to be the reason anything bad could happen to anyone.

He nods, his face looks grim. "We'd love to have you over again this week for dinner."

I smile. "I'll let you know once Luis puts out the new schedule."

"Adios," he says, tilting his hat before leaving.

"What time are you done?" Jay asks.

"I might close," I tell him noncommittally.

"Blaise." He bites my name out. The muscles in his forearms ripple under the flannel button-up, and his anger flashes across his face.

"Not right now, Jarrod," I warn him. We're at an impasse and I refuse to break first. With a shake of his head, he turns and leaves without a word. I let go of the breath I had been holding when I catch Luis watching me.

"What?" I ask him, all my anger gone, and I feel deflated again.

"You worked seven days in a row, kid. Go home," he tells me.

"I'm filling in since you're down a server, remember?" I laugh.

"I can cover the bar. You need to rest. You're scaring my customers." He nods to old man Mitchel at the end of the bar, who holds his hands up in surrender when I shoot my gaze to him.

"I filled your drink every time," I tell him, hiding the laughter in my voice. Mitchel was a regular and never complained about anyone.

"You want me to leave that badly?" I ask Luis, wringing my hand on the towel. In all the years I've worked for him, Luis has never sent me home. His features soften and concern seeps into his eyes.

"You're a hard worker, Blaise, but even I know right now you need a break. Go home and sleep," he tells me, shrugging.

"You sure?" I ask again before grabbing my bag from under the bar. He nods.

I don't wait for him to change his mind. Now that I know Jay and the guys are back, my body is ready to shut down. I make it to my car and somehow I make it home. I don't remember the drive, my muscle memory doing all the work for me. My bed welcomes me like a tight hug pulling me in.

———————

Sweat has gathered on my neck as I unwind myself from my blanket. An annoying buzz still pounding in my ears. I rub my eyes, feeling disoriented, unsure of the time and what day it is. My hand reaches for the phone under my pillow just as the vibrations stop.

5 missed calls Jay

15 messages

My eyes are wide awake now. It's five past eleven when I was supposed to leave. Ignoring the missed calls, I go through my texts and open the two from Toni.

Jay: (10)

Stone: ...

Joe:...

Toni: Stone said you're coming tonight?

I can pick you up. On my way now ;)

Jenna: ....

"Shit!" I quickly jump out of bed and run to the bathroom. My hair is a disaster and gross, drool is dried to the corner of my lip. "Lovely," I whisper to myself before grabbing a washcloth and scrubbing my face and neck. Running back to my room, I whip off Jay's t-shirt I had fallen asleep in, before pulling on my favorite pair of fishnet tights, destroyed jean shorts, and black crop top sweater. My phone now reads ten after eleven and Toni will be here any minute. I quickly tip my head over and gather all my hair up into a messy ponytail on top of my head. I grab my favorite mascara off the dresser, fixing what I had put on earlier. My feet slide into my black combat boots right as there is a knock on the front door.

"Blaise!" I hear Toni yell from the other side.

"Just a sec!" I yell back, frantically shoving my arms into my leather jacket.

Thrusting the deadbolt out of the way, I almost crashed right into Toni.

"Whoa!" He laughs. "Are you okay?"

"Fine." I shrug, following him out into the cool air. "Just overslept."

"I figured something happened when you didn't respond right away. Hope it's okay I just showed up," he tells me as we get into his car.

"It's fine," I reassure him. "Sorry I didn't respond. Luis sent me home early. I meant to take a short nap, but I must have been more tired than I thought."

"It's all good." He smiles at me, the dim light from the dashboard lighting up his face. "The guys are already on their way there. Joe might be racing as a fill-in. Not sure yet."

"Okay." I smile back, trying to calm my breathing down. My phone vibrates again in my pocket and I ignore it. Toni's eyes slide to me, but he doesn't say anything. True to form Toni cranks on System Of A Down's "Chop Suey" while speeding out of town toward the desert.

Scar is lit up, the variety of headlights dotting across the area mirroring the image of the night sky. The bass in the background reaches us before we even cross over the peak and head toward the crowd. Any sense of being tired completely vanishes as the excitement washes over me.

"Beer?" Toni asks, handing me an unopen can from his backpack.

"Sure," I say, taking it and appreciating the fact it was somewhat still cold. We walk our way through the crowd to the familiar group of people by the sidelines.

"Nah," Joey says, scratching his hand through his hair. "It shouldn't make that click noise when you downshift."

"I agree," a guy next to him replies.

"Do we have time to get that part changed?" Stone asks them, leaning over the car now as well.

"I don't know?" Joey leans back, looking exasperated. "If we send Jerome to talk to Lion, maybe we could get an extra, but it would cost us."

"Do it." Stone nods with authority. The other guy backs up from the car and pulls a phone out of his pocket.

"Issues already?" Toni asks. They all turn to us, noticing we just arrived.

"Hey, little B," Joey says before throwing his arm around me in a side hug. I sink into him briefly while nodding at Stone who acknowledges me with a salute, still leaning over the car.

"They'll figure it out," I tell Toni. I'm very confident in Joey's ability to fix a car. His brain works wonders around anything mechanical.

"We should talk before Jerome gets back," Stone announces. I feel Joey tense next to me. My eyes catch Toni's and a flicker of fear sparks in his.

I clear my throat. "I just got a really weird text from Seth. I'm worried about him. I know you guys said you hadn't heard from him. It just freaked me out." I watch as Stone's gaze flits over the guys. His brain working rapidly. I didn't lie per se.

"What exactly did he say?" Stone asks me.

"It didn't say anything. Just something about loyalty?" I lie this time. Seth's cryptic message did scare me. The fact that he clearly has a new cell phone and is still hiding freaks me out. What scares me the most though is that he is right. I shouldn't trust anyone. The only person I trusted with my life is no longer here and his death is a giant question mark.

"He's off his rocker since Blake," Joey says quietly, pulling me closer to him in a hug.

"We all didn't handle it well, but it hit Seth extra hard. They'd known each other since elementary," Toni responds, his eyes glazing over.

"I wouldn't put much thought into it," Stone replies, shrugging. "If he keeps bothering you though, let me know." I nod. The mood around us shifts, each of us lost in our own thoughts. My body starts to relax when I feel Joey give me another squeeze causing me to look up at him.

"What the hell is that?" Toni practically growls. My head whips in his direction, but he's looking behind me. I slowly turn, trying to maneuver out of Joey's grip. I still as an angry flush spreads over my chest up to my brain, which is shortcircuiting. A red haze clouds my vision while dread fills my stomach. Jay arrived, and he wasn't alone. A leggy brunette was attached at his hip. She was dressed impeccably in designer jeans, Ugg boots, and a name brand pink jacket. I recognized her from around town. She usually stopped into Locos with a group of people on Saturdays. The college crowd, we called them. His arm was draped across her shoulders and she held his dangling hand.

"Blaisey," Joey says next to my ear, trying to get my attention, but it's no use. I'm transfixed on the sight in front of me. My eyes shoot daggers at the chick by Jay's side. When my blues clash with his brown eyes, I swear his flash with triumph.

Come here he mouths, not taking his gaze from mine. I raise my eyebrow at him, tilting my chin before giving him my back.

"Asshole," I mutter to myself, trying to push back the burn of tears.

"Want us to kill him? Maybe maim him or something?" Joey asks, leaning down. His face looks serious, but I can read the playfulness in his tone. I smile, ignoring the vibrating from my phone in my pocket.

"Not today. Just kick their asses in the race." I nod toward the car.

"That won't be a problem." Toni laughs before closing the hood. He steps back and comes to stand next to me. Joey gives me a final squeeze before jumping into the driver's seat. We watch as he pulls away and gets situated at the starting line.

"That's a badass car," Stone murmurs next to me, but I'm not paying attention.

With the race starting, I now have a clear line of sight on Jay and the girl again. She's burrowed into his side, chatting away happily. She doesn't even seem to notice that he's not paying attention. We're locked in a silent battle. His arm drops from her shoulders and settles down to her waist, his hand flexing at her side. I shudder, remembering how it feels to have his hands at my waist, his fingers gripping me tightly.

Phone, he mouths to me and I shake my head. He's baiting me to do what he wants and I'm not falling for it. His eyes narrow, the brown turning almost black. He's pissed. He dips his head down until his lips are a whisper away from her neck. Pain slices across my chest. I tear my eyes away, forcing myself to pay attention to what is happening on the track instead.

"How many people are racing tonight?" I ask Stone.

"Three more after Joe's," he responds, never taking his gaze from the car. I nod again and push myself to watch. No surprise that Joey is leading again and will probably win. I don't feel in the mood to be here anymore though. I allow myself another glance and find Jay and her still cozied up.

"I need some air… fumes, you know," I tell Stone who just nods, barely paying me any attention.

"I'm going up to the lookout," I tell Toni, who smiles and nods at me.

After making my way out of the crowd, I find the ledge and follow it up to the peak called the Look Out. From here I can see the race below and more of the track as it disappears around the corner. No crowd and the chill from the fall breeze cools the simmering heat beneath my skin. The solitude is comforting.

"Palmer, right?" a deep voice speaks next to me. I watch as he walks out of the shadows before leaning his long form against the boulder next to me. His dirty blonde hair is long on top and cropped short on the sides. The tight white t-shirt he wears under a yellow and black riding jacket pulls tightly against his chest. A few swirls of dark ink underneath can be seen through the material. His jaw is square and hard. The smile on his full pink lips matches the laugh, and his baby blues are the color of the ocean.

"Do I know you?" I ask, feigning boredom. This dude looks like the all –American dream boy turned bad-boy.

"Probably not," he says, laughing, the sound is deep and warm. "I see you're running with the Baby-Face crew." He nods down below us.

"Who?" I question, completely confused.

"Did you pay attention in history class?" he asks before taking a cigarette from his jacket and lighting up. I shrug in response. "Baby Face Nelson was a leader of a gang in the 30s. They robbed banks and were murderers."

"Why was he called Baby Face?" I ask, playing along.

"His face had a youthful look. He was young," the guy says, shrugging. "Just like Stone, Antonio, and Joseph."

I laugh. "They're hardly a gang," I tell him, smirking.

His head cocks to the side. "You really don't know, do you?" he asks, a hint of a smile curving his mouth. I let my face fall blank, refusing to answer. "Everyone at this track has their hands in something illegal, Blaise. It's why they come here. Drugs, guns, illegal racing, betting, gambling, money. It's how this place thrives."

"I just come here to watch my friends race," I tell him, not sure who I'm really defending.

His eyes slide over me, questions bouncing back and forth in his brain. "True. Those guys though… They're a big deal in Vegas."

Now, it's my turn to laugh again. "They work at a hotel."

"Sure," he says, smirking. I'm really starting to not like this guy.

"And, you would know how?" I demand.

"Blake," he says, dropping my brother's name in the space between us. My mouth slams shut. "Doesn't McCall tell you anything?"

"Hardly," I tell him, annoyed. "You know Jay, too?" I ask, biting my lip.

"You could say that. We're all friends, sort of." He scratches his head with his free hand, flicking ashes with the other. "We're friends. I was in high school when I first met McCall. I helped him by being his informant. Fucked up my race career in the end, but it helped stop many drug dealers and murderers, so I guess it was worth it," he replies before taking a long drag. His story starts to click in my brain. Memories of Blake telling me the story about the motocross racer who was framed with drug charges by his girlfriend. It was the second offense and even though he was proven innocent, he still lost his career. He went off the map after that. He was rumored to be in illegal activities as a 'fuck you' to the system. Blake spoke of him like they were friends.

My eyes wander farther over the guy, resting on his knuckles where SCAR was inked. "You're Trent Nichols," I say, rather than ask.

He winks at me. "You're Blake's little sister. I've heard a lot about you."

"How?" My voice is thick with emotion, strangling my vocal cords.

"We both knew McCall. Spent a lot of time together working out the case," he answers.

My shoulders fall. "You're a cop?"

"Sometimes." He shrugs. Undercover. "Been doing this for a while. There never seems to be an end point to this case. Drugs always seem to pop up. New rulers soon follow and a wake of bodies are left behind. That's why I'm here to tell you not to trust anyone. Not even the ones you feel most loyal to."

"Can I trust Jay?" I ask the question that's been heaviest on my heart. Our eyes connect, and I know Trent can read all my secrets and what Jay means to me. His head falls back. He breathes out a cloud of smoke before flicking his cigarette to the ground.

"Blake did," Trent answers. "In my experience though, don't trust anybody. It's the best way to stay alive."

Tears blur my vision. Alone again, I let them fall silently down my face. I have no idea which way is up. Who is the enemy and who is on my side? I'm on my own and I feel like I'm being pulled in half between my past and my future. I want to cry and scream out all the pain and agony that's been trapped inside me for the past six months. Out here in the desert, in the middle of nowhere, where no one would witness the epic meltdown that I was harboring.

Trent…Don't trust anyone.

Seth…Don't trust anyone.

Jay…Trust me.

Picking myself up from off the rock, I slide my fingers across my cheeks, destroying the evidence that a single tear fell. Trent is long gone and the noise from the crowd below only signals what I already knew would happen. The race was over and Joey won. I just don't have it in me to be excited anymore. I slide my phone out of my pocket and ignore the three more calls and ten texts from Jay. Shooting a quick text to Toni, I let him know I'm not feeling good and heading home early. After the good head fuck, my stomach is a roiling mass of queasiness. So, it's not a lie. I shoot another text to Joey congratulating him on the win. Once I make it to the road, I realize what a dumbass move that was as I arrived with Toni.

"Great," I mutter to myself, trying to decide if the walk is worth it or if I could run in these boots. My body comes to a halt at the rev of a bike engine right as it pulls up in front of me, cutting off my path. Jay balances the machine between his legs and wordlessly hands me the extra black helmet from the back.

My fingers brush the hard plastic hesitantly before firmly taking it and sliding it over my head. I grip Jay's jacket while slinging my leg over the seat. The design of the motorbike stations my seat higher, forcing me forward into Jay's body. I wrap my arms around his middle and lay my head at his back. There is no use fighting gravity in this situation. Jay takes off and brings us back into town, past the main street shopping and bars, past the two churches, and post office before turning onto my street. When he parks and cuts the engine, I scramble off the seat, gently lobbing the helmet onto the back.

"Thanks," I offer before speed walking to my door. Jay moves stealth-like and I don't hear him behind me until it's too late. He grips my arms and swings me around until my back hits the door, and we're standing chest to chest. He's breathing heavily, his eyes shining in the darkness around us.

"Let me in," he says quietly. His voice gravelly to my ears.

"Where's your new flavor?" I tip my head to the side while attempting to bring my hand to his chest.

"Did I get your attention?" he asks, his jaw clenched. Blood surges to my cheeks when I remember the flare of jealousy and possessiveness I felt with his arm wrapped around her.

"That's all she was," he tells me, his hands gripping the sides of my face. "I lost her the minute I couldn't find you anymore."

"Don't play games with me," I warn him, my fingers gripping his wrists. Heat flashes in his eyes.

"Stop fighting me. I'm not going anywhere. I can't always tell you everything right away because I don't want to lie to you. You're already in way too deep and I'm not putting your life on the line. Trust me," he demands before he smashes his mouth down to mine, lifting my body into his at the same time.

I struggle on my tiptoes and I'm forced to grip his jacket for balance. The sharp intake of breath is the perfect opportunity for Jay to push his tongue into my mouth. This kiss is fierce and intoxicatingly different than when he's kissed me before. It's not claiming, but staking his ownership. His lips push and pull against mine, teeth bite at the sensitive part of my lower lip, and I can't stop the moan that leaks out. It's all Jay needed though. He has the door open and is back on me before I can question how the hell he got past the locks. This time I meet him pull for push. My hands greedily shove his jacket off and before gripping the ends of his button-up shirt and ripping it open. The tinkling of buttons hitting the floor sounds sexy and does crazy things to me. It's only a matter of time before I'm gripping the scorching bare skin on his back. Jay's boots crunch over the scattered buttons before he grips my sides and hauls me onto the countertop. My mind briefly recalls that my mom is gone and won't come home to witness this before Jay is yanking my sweater off over my head. His lips move in hot trails down the sensitive skin of my neck to my collarbone.

"Where did you go?" he asks, pulling my leg up and unlacing the boot on my foot.

"Huh?" I question, not sure I heard him right.

"Where did you go during the race?" he clarifies, untying my other boot. They both hit the floor with a thump. His long fingers hook on my belt loops, pulling my body closer to the edge. "Hmm, Blaise?" His eyes bore into mine, my mind is still fighting through the haze trying to piece together the information he wants. My heart thudded in my chest with the realization that he was watching me. I just want his lips back on me.

The zipper on my shorts is pulled down, and I gasped at the sensation when my bare skin lands on the cold granite. I bite my lip, smirking. "The Look Out," I tell him breathlessly, reaching down to unclasp his jeans. The growl that leaves his mouth causes goosebumps to raise on my skin. Wrapping my arms around his neck, my mouth battles with his, while my feet push his jeans off his hips and down his legs.

"Jay," I whisper against his lips, a plea to end the yearning in my chest.

"Stop running from me, baby," he rasps against my lips, brushing his fingers against my center. "Trust me."

Air leaves my lungs when he plunges two fingers inside me, curling and stroking to match the thrust from my hips. My head falls back, my body racked from the sensations he's creating. Before I can come undone, Jay withdraws from my body, teasing, keeping me on edge.

"Please." Leaves my lips, I sound breathless and I hate that he has me almost pleading. I'm not even sure what I'm asking for. Answers? Trust? Protection? To just fucking finish me already?

I don't miss the curl of his lip before he violently slams into me. My hands flutter at his shoulders, my nails digging in, holding on. Jay's grip on my hips tighten, bringing my hips back to meet his with every thrust. I know I'll have bruises on the insides of my thighs in the morning and I don't care. There is something deliciously territorial about it. I wrapped one arm around Jay's neck and use the other to grip the lip of the countertop as leverage to anchor my body. My orgasm builds again, stronger and more intense each time Jay's cock hits that special spot deep inside.

"You going to come for me, baby?" Jay rasps out, his grip on my thigh tightening while his fingers on his other hand pinch and pull at my nipples. Biting my lip, I nod frantically. I might kill him if he stops again like before. I need the release only Jay can give me. "Are you going to be a good girl and come all over my cock?" His words are dirty and thrill me at the same time. "Answer me, Blaise." My name sounds scratchy as it flows from his mouth, which only heightens my own pleasure. I'm getting to him, too.

"Yes," I answer, watching the color of his brown eyes deepen to dark molten chocolate.

"You like it when I control your body like this, don't you, Blaise?" He grins wickedly, I'm close and he's keeping it out of reach, playing with me.

"Yes." The word falls from my mouth, my brain clearly not connecting to my pussy anymore. His hand slides up until my neck is cradled against his palm when he squeezes. My body shudders from the threat of losing oxygen, only amping up the impending tidal wave of sensation I'm on the brink of. My eyes widen, my lips part in a silent plea. I don't like it when Jay takes control... I love it. I'm not telling him that though. Our eyes connect while he continues to squeeze and release my neck, controlling my breathing. The moment he lets me find my release, his grip tightens with every last thrust from his hips, pushing wave after wave of my orgasm through me. My toes curl and my hands slide off his shoulders from the beaded sweat.

"I love when you do that," Jay says breathlessly.

"Hmm?" I respond, not able to comprehend anything. My naked body now leaning into him, the minute my legs drop down his sides it feels like pins and needles. I follow his gaze and notice visible inch long red scratch marks over his shoulder blades. My cheeks instantly heat pink.

"Not sorry," I mutter. He laughs.

"Let's get to your room."

I shake my head. "I don't want to move."

"Hold on," Jay says before sliding out and readjusting his jeans back over his hips. He kicks off his shoes before scooping me off the counter.

"My clothes," I remind him, laughing.

"They'll be fine till tomorrow morning," he responds, maneuvering us down the hall to my room. I'm about to remind him that I'm not the only one who lives here, but I stop when I remember her latest note. It said she won't be back for a while. Nothing else.

Jay tosses me onto the mattress before setting his gun on the nightstand. My eyes follow every movement of muscle while he lets his jeans fall to the ground beside my bed.

"Be right back." He winks before heading to my bathroom. Exhausted, my body collapses back on the bed.

"The fuck?" I mutter to myself. The night took a complete one-eighty in a matter of an hour. I was about ready to write Jay off and now he's in my apartment again staying the night. Trent's words play over in my head. *Blake did.* My brother trusted Jay. Jay wanted me to trust him, but he wasn't telling me everything yet and that wasn't something I was okay with.

Getting up off my bed, I swipe a t-shirt from the drawer and slide it over my now tangled hair, down my body.

"Where were you?" I demand, sliding into the bathroom behind him. Our eyes connect in the mirror while he brushes his teeth. *When did he even bring a toothbrush over?* I don't look away and neither does he. Blue toothpaste foams out of the corner of his mouth before he spits, rinses, and then turns to face me.

"Vegas," he answers instantly. His eyes dart over my face, watching intently.

"No shit? Why?"

"There was a lead that the group of people we had been previously out to set up were going to be there for another run," he replies.

"Why didn't you answer my text?"

"I leave my personal phone in my locker when I'm in deep." He shrugs. "If I get caught, they have less leverage to press me with."

"You were back early though. You know how freaked out I was. Why did you wait so long to come see me?" I ask, allowing myself to be vulnerable to this man.

"I was waiting..." Guilt flashed in his eyes quickly, but it was there. "I was waiting to see what their priority was after. If there were additional contacts that needed to be made or if that was just the end. If they just kept the money and went about life again."

The blood leaves my face while a chill creeps over my skin. My eyes slam shut while my lungs struggle to bring air in and out. "Do I need to worry about the guys?" I grit out between clenched teeth.

Jay looks away from me, cracking his knuckles. His shoulders lift in a shrug. The look on his face giving nothing away.

"I'm not sure, yet? I felt even worse coming back to see you because I have nothing concrete to give you. Only more questions and another dead end. I've been working this case for almost four years and it's just as fucked now as it was in the beginning. I know the little people. I know their game. I know the big players at the top. I just don't…" His voice trails off. Jay looks defeated, leaning against my sink.

In two steps, I wrap my arms around his waist, breathing in the faint smell of diesel from the track that still lingers on his skin. "There never seems to be an endpoint to this case. Drugs always seem to pop up. New rulers soon follow, and a wake of bodies are left behind," I repeat.

Jay freezes in my hold. "I ran into Trent Nichols at the race. It's why I left," I tell him, pulling his body closer to mine until I feel the tension in his muscles leave, molding us together again.

"Great." He half laughs and half cringes. "He's right though. Every time I get close to figuring it all out, it's like they disappear into thin air. Only Blake had it figured out and he's not here anymore." We both stand in silence, our thoughts millions of miles apart yet still bound together with a common interest.

"You'll figure it out," I tell him. "Blake trusted you enough to help you. Hell, you changed his whole life around. I had no idea he wanted to be a police officer, let alone he was going to school. He wouldn't invest that much into someone or something unless he had faith in it, in them. You'll get it."

Jay's arms tighten around my body, prompting me to lift my head up. The look in his eyes steals my breath away. "You're amazing, Blaise," he whispers against my lips before sealing our mouths together in a kiss that leaves me flushed and my legs weak.

Jay walks us back to my room and onto my bed before sliding

in and pulling me to his side. I fall asleep listening to the slowing beat of Jay's heart. I decide right there and then to try and let go and trust him. I can't be as cynical as Trent, but I figure he has his own reasons for being how he is. The most important person in my life, the one person who loved me unconditionally and gave their all for me trusted Jay, or at the very least for the cause that Jay is fighting. For now, that would have to be enough.

Ten

"WHAT'S UP?" I ASK, PLACING THE DRINKS down in front of them. "I know you didn't call me over here because my face is prettier than Jenna's," I joke. Their solemn expressions freak me out. Chills sprinkle across my arms from Jay's warning.

"What's up with you and the mechanic?" Joey asks.

My shoulders lift. "Not much," I respond, keeping my face neutral. Inside, my hackles are raised in defense.

"He called you his girlfriend," Antonio states.

I swing my gaze to his. "Didn't know you gossiped like a woman, Toni. Should I get you a frothy glass to go with that bottle?" My words are icy. At least he has some decency to break eye contact first. Part of me also wants to smack Jay for letting that slip. He stopped in for an early dinner, as he called it. I knew he was watching the guys. The only problem is they're starting to notice him more. Before he left, Jay had leaned over the bar, claiming my lips in front of the whole restaurant. If that hadn't been bad enough, he turned to Luis and handed him some cash.

"For my girlfriend's tip." He winked and grinned, not hiding his laugh on his way out the door.

"It's not our business—" Stone starts to reply, but I cut him off.

"Damn straight, it's not."

"You haven't been in a relationship since Seth," Joey reminds me. I roll my eyes as I remind them. "That was over two years ago, I didn't know that meant I could never date again."

"We're just concerned," Toni throws out there like it makes their meddling any better.

"Why?" I ask, my voice louder than intended. "What I do has nothing to do with you guys anymore. You made sure of that, remember?" It's a low blow, but it hits the mark like I intended. Joey looks away, his jaw clenched. Toni's head drops into his hands while Stone just stares at me like always. "Look, guys," I tell them, taking a deep breath. "I appreciate that you're concerned, but you don't have to be. I'm a big girl. And whatever is happening with Jay and me, is between us. It's too new to tell anyway."

"We didn't mean to say you couldn't fend for yourself, B. It's just… Blake would ask questions too… ya know?" Joey states. I barely hear the choke in his words, but it's there. Tears instantly spring to my eyes. Blake would have been all over my ass asking questions if I'm completely honest. Most of the time he liked to razz me, but he also took his role as big brother seriously. My gaze scans the faces of the guys we grew up with while a small pit of guilt starts to grow in my chest. Jay's words are fresh in my mind, yet as I look around the booth, it's too easy to see my brother sitting on the end. His eyes blazing with humor, his posture defensive. He would know he was being unreasonable, but wouldn't give a fuck because I'm his baby sister. He would grin his cocky half-smile because whatever poor sucker I was interested in would have to deal with all of them.

"I know," I respond, feeling the watery path of a tear stream down my cheek. I quickly swipe it away with my free hand. "I got it though," I tell them reassuringly.

"We know," Stone replies. "It's just hard to turn those protective instincts off when it comes to you, little Palmer." He shrugs while the guys chuckle. "We actually really wanted to let you know that we're going back to Vegas again next weekend."

"Already?" I ask. "Didn't you just get back?"

"Yeah. It's promising to be a good weekend though," Stone replies, nodding.

"Ya know it!" Toni whoops. "Gotta love it when La Mamacita decides to play."

"Dude." Joey laughs and shoves him playfully.

"Anyway," Stone says, shooting him a look. "We wanted to see if you wanted to come with. Like old times."

Their invitation hangs in the air between us. Three pairs of eyes and one haunting gaze waiting for my reaction. I force a smile to my lips despite the nagging feeling in my stomach. The conversation with Jay is fresh in my mind, yet the guilt for doubting them is eating at me. The least that could happen would be that I get some information for Jay to clear the guys from his shit list.

"Yeah, I would really like that, actually," I answer before I overthink it.

"Yes!" Toni laughs, giving me a fist bump. They each get out of the booth one by one and give me a hug. Stone slaps money on the table before turning to me. "Just leave your boy at home though, Palmer." I nod even while a sliver of unease slides through my stomach.

I watch while they head out the front door, wondering what I have done. I glance back at the booth. In my mind, Blake sits there, shaking his head, his eyes frustrated. I lift my shoulder in a shrug. "I can help," I whisper out loud despite being alone. I've never been more determined than ever to get to the bottom of this case and give my brother the peace he needs. On cue, The Black Crows' song "She Talks To Angels" starts to play from the speakers. My chest feels heavy when I look back at the booth and only empty glasses and dishes are waiting for me. My pocket vibrates and I pull my cell phone out only to find a text from Jay.

Jay: New shipment of parts arrived this afternoon. I'm staying late to help so Rowland can get home to watch his baby tonight.

Me: K. See you tomorrow?

Jay: ;)

Sighing, I clear the rest of the dishes off the table and head back to the bar. My plans for the night now uncertain. At the same time, I feel relieved after, in a roundabout way, I betrayed Jay. Which was ridiculous, but my heart still felt heavy, anyways.

I finish my shift methodically under Luis' watchful eye. The minute I have my payout and I'm in the car driving home, I start to plan my run for the evening. It's been a while since I've had the time or the energy to get back out there. I change quickly and grab my earbuds before hitting the pavement. Ignoring the first twinges in my shins, I push away the pain, forcing my chest to find an even breathing pace. By mile two, the familiarity is back and I'm numb from the waist down. Collective Soul's "Shine" drums in my head while my brain and my conscience battle out the dilemma I've put myself into. After circling the town, my legs are rubbery, the tank I threw on is molded to my torso with sweat. I've finally made it back, yet I still have no answers. No clarity and I'm beginning to feel like a major fuck up.

Clicking on my fan, I take off my sweaty socks and just as I am about to pull my tank over my head, a movement in my peripheral causes my adrenaline to spike. "Shit," I mumble, stepping back in time to witness the shadow by my window move. Reaching blindly for the baseball bat behind my door, I inch closer to the window just as his face pressed closer, attempting to look into my room. *Seth.* Frozen in panic, I hold my breath, watching him hold a hand up to shield the glare from the streetlight while he searches the room for me. I pause before he raps his knuckles gently in succession against the glass pane. Tap-Tap-Ta-ta-tap. Not waiting, I charge the window and yanked it open, surprising him.

"Whoa!" Seth lets out, losing his balance and tumbles halfway through the opening.

"What the hell!" I shout at the same time.

"Shh!" He pulls himself through the rest of the way before shutting the window and relocking it. Even in the seventy-degree temps at night, Seth is way overdressed in dark black cargo pants and a black hoodie His usually wavy brown hair and sun-kissed face is hidden under the bill of his all black baseball cap.

"What are you—" I start to ask before his hand cups over my mouth and his free arm pulls my body into his. He checks out the window, scoping out the ground below before moving us farther into my room to the closet.

I shake my head violently, struggling in his grip. Everyone's accusations and questioning Seth's disappearance the past month are fresh and send shockwaves of fear through my body.

"Chill, Blaise," he whispers against my cheek. "I'm not going to hurt you." I stop struggling and let my body go limp in his grasp. "Is he here?" Seth asks, watching me closely, seeing the confusion flick over my face. "McCall?" Seth presses further. I stiffen in his arms, wondering if I should lie and tell him that Jay will be here soon, even though Jay isn't actually coming. I'm torn between calling him and wanting to beat Seth with my baseball bat until he tells me where the fuck he's been, and what the mystery is around him. I shake my head no, noticing the way Seth visibly relaxes. His arm slides off my waist and his hand falls from my mouth.

"How do you know about Jay?" I ask, wiping the salty taste from Seth's palm off my lips.

Seth's eyebrow lifts. "Jay?" He laughs. "Seriously?"

"Seriously, what?" I ask him angrily. All the pent up frustration I've been holding inside for months pushes forward, ready to rear her ugly head. "You think you get to fucking come to my house, attack me and question me? You fucked up big time, Seth. Everyone is looking for you. They want answers and I do, too. I thought we meant something to you? I thought we were family, but Blake dies and what... you run out of town under mysterious circumstances and everyone starts tracking me down like I'm your keeper! What the fuck is that!"

"It isn't like that, Blaise," he groans, frustrated, pulling the hat from his head and sitting on my bed. I watch as he cradles his head, and his shoulders bounce slightly. "Are you on a first-name basis with the guy?"

"Are you crying?" I demand.

"Answer the question," he responds.

"Yes," I tell him, lifting my arms in defeat. "Who cares?"

"Are you fucking?" he questions, and I don't miss the hint of disgust in his voice. I remain silent. "Guess that answers that then."

"Where have you been?" I fire off. "Why is everyone looking for you?"

Seth looks up at me. Even in the dim light in the room, I can see his eyes are rimmed red, dark circles highlighted under his spiky bottom lashes. "I don't know what else to do." His throat bobs when he swallows, wetness glistens in his green eyes. "Shit went down and it wasn't good. He… he was dead before I could do anything. He tried to text me, but I was too late to get the warning."

"So, you took what they needed and left?" I push him further, pretty sure my blood pressure was through the roof.

"I just grabbed the bag like Blake told me to." Seth's shoulders drop in defeat. "Did you get my text?"

"I don't know," I answer sarcastically. "Are you 'unknown caller?'"

"I'm serious, Blaise, you can't trust any of them." Seth stands again, facing me.

"Why should I trust a goddamn word that comes out of your mouth, Seth? Where were you? I needed you. You left and they've been here," I vent.

His eyes searching mine, the familiar deep green orbs spilling tears and secrets.

"I couldn't stay with everyone looking for me. I didn't know who to trust anymore. Blake said where to find the bag and told me to run. It was all a setup. He was trying to protect me," he explains.

"Who set him up?" I asked breathlessly.

"I don't know. That's why I said not to trust anyone. Not the guys and not McCall." Seth gets up quickly and heads to my window in three strides, scanning the ground and across the street, keeping his body tucked into my curtains and the shadows. "Look, I don't have a lot of time. I didn't hear from you and I wanted to make sure you're okay. This whole thing is fucked, Blaise. You need to listen to me though. I know you don't trust me, I know I haven't been here, but it's not because I don't want to be. It killed me not to be with you for the funeral. My best friend in the entire world is gone and he shouldn't be. Don't trust anyone. Record everything. It's all about money. Go back to Scar and ask Trent about Mamacita. He'll put it together. Hand me your phone."

"No," I tell him, stepping back, clutching my cell closer to my chest, "Who is Mamacita? What does that mean?"

He takes my phone effortlessly before I can protest then hands it back. "Do not repeat that name to anyone, got it? Only Trent. I know you met him."

"How do you…" I feel the blood leave my face. "Oh my god, are you spying on me?"

Seth's head tilts back with a laugh. "That's fuckin' hilarious considering who you're in bed with. No, I don't have to fucking stalk you, Blaise. Trent texted me. Ask him if you aren't sure."

"Why would he talk to you?" I question. "I thought he was a cop and was working with Jay, I mean McCall."

Seth grunts. "Trent doesn't work for anyone. He's in so deep even he doesn't know which end is up anymore. Go talk to him more. Then text me."

"I don't have your number," I remind him, a smug smile pulls at my lips.

"You do now," he tells me before flipping the lock and popping my window up. I blink and he's completely gone. I flip on my light and make my way over to the window. There is no sign of him on the fire escape or below. Closing my eyes, I inhale the evening desert air and breathe out while counting to five. When my eyes slide open, I glance around the room. The imprint of where Seth had sat on my bed is still there, meaning it wasn't my imagination looking for answers.

"I should have run longer," I mumble to myself, closing the window and locking it before yanking the curtain shut. I move over to my bedroom door and lock that, too, before sliding under my covers with the baseball bat, cuddling up to it for safety. My fingers hover over the screen, tempted to text Jay to come over after work. Seth's warnings freak me out. He looked like shit and to be honest, everything he told me felt sincere.

"What should I do?" I whisper into the darkness of my room. Closing my eyes, I can see Blake leaning against my bed, sitting in the same spot Seth just vacated. His face is concerned because he knows. He knows the answer, but can't tell me. Light shines behind my eyeballs and I crack one eye open to find my phone lit up. Blood pounds in my ears when I lift the screen to my face.

Jay: How was your shift? Are you in bed yet?

I exhale the air from my lungs before typing out an answer.

Me: It was long but the usual. Yes, I'm in bed :)

Me: Are you still at work?

Jay: Yup. There are a shit ton of parts and of course they sent some of the wrong ones so we've had to catalog those.

Jay: I would rather be with you

Me: I would rather you be here too ;)

Jay: Hang out tomorrow?

Me: Text me when you wake up.

Jay. K. Night babe

Me: Night :)

Sleep that night was more exhausting than being awake. Every dream was me chasing Seth or me driving after Blake only to end at the same place over and over again. Instead of Blake's car around the tree, it's mine and all Jay can say at my funeral was that I trusted the wrong people. My heart is pounding, my shirt was drenched in sweat when I wake up. My eyes adjust to the light filtering through the room. The air is stale and sticky, making me question what time it is, and what woke me up from a dead sleep. My hand slides to my phone on the nightstand.

1 New Message glares back at me. I tap the screen open and bring up my messages.

Boyfriend #2: I meant what I said. I'm sorry. I would have been there if I could have been. Remember what I told you. Stay Smart.

I glare at the text. I guess it wasn't a dream and is just my own messed-up reality. I slump back against my pillows wishing the bed would swallow me whole. This situation continues to get more complicated every day. I check my phone again, also noticing that there are no new messages from Jay. My pulse kicks up. My heart is filled with shame and I can't shake the small slice of betrayal pie I'm feeding to Jay. I'm ready for answers. I don't want to be the dumb girl in the horror movie that stays home because her boyfriend is protecting her, then she ends up dying anyway because the bad guy was plotting the entire time for when she is alone. It's a cliché I want no part of. The asshole who killed my brother will pay. The innocent will be protected and I will finally move on.

Eleven

IT WAS EASY. THE LIES THAT FELL from my tongue were too easy. Jay believed I was going with Jenna and Molly to visit UNLV for the weekend. That I was finally taking those steps to being independent again and planning for a future. He went on and on about how it was perfect timing and he would be busy working between Sarge's ranch and the shop to keep up appearances. I packed my bag without sweating over it. I even left my mom a note with the same lie. Hell, I told it so many times this week that even I almost believed it. Everything fell into place like I had planned. I was cramped in the back seat with Antonio while Joe sat shotgun and Stone drove us the couple hours north to the Vegas strip. They were going to work at the newest hotel and casino on the strip, La Flor. A single text from Seth sat unopened in my inbox. I hadn't had time to seek out Trent like he suggested and frankly, I had no reason to believe either of them. My gut told me that what I needed to know I was going to find in Las Vegas.

"Sin City," I whispered when the neon lights from the Strip were starting to glow in the early evening dusk and could be seen from my small vantage point in the back.

"Where demons hide." Antonio wags his brows at me, a look of excitement and knowing crosses his face. My breath catches and I play it off quickly like his words don't send shivers down my spine.

"Where millionaires fall and the underdog can become someone," Joe adds from the front seat before rolling down his window and letting his hand coast through the air.

"Where the depraved can be left in peace while the weak-minded are held accountable." Stone joins their twisted word game. I fight the urge to roll my eyes, not fully understanding where the conversation is going. Believing they sound like coked-up frat boys on their first weekend of rush at college, only they've already been graduated for fifteen years, and now they're the creepy guys at the bar. Seriously?

"Er," I hesitate. "Are we staying at this hotel, too, or just working?" It's been a few years since I've been on a Vegas run and even then, I never had a hand in the actual planning. The guys had the jobs lined up, and Blake took care of the hotel, sometimes plural, that we stayed at.

"Yup," Antonio replies, using his index finger to poke my forehead. "No worries, B, it's all taken care of."

"Things are going to seem a little different this time, Blaisey," Joe warns me, turning in his seat to meet my eyes. "We're pretty well known in these parts."

"What he means to say," Stone interjects, his deep black eyes finding mine in the rearview mirror. "Is it's less manual labor now. And we usually celebrate at the club afterward these days."

"In style," Joe throws in there, smirking proudly.

"Oh," I tell them. "I didn't bring anything to go out in."

"We'll take care of it," Stone assures me. "I'm sure one of the girls will have something you can borrow."

I nod along and put a plastic smile on my lips, not wanting to be a bitch, but the idea of borrowing a dress from a random chick to wear to a Vegas nightclub is not appealing. Deciding not to argue, I sit back in my seat and watch the scenery fly past me. I could people-watch on the Strip all day long. Such a variety of humans live and vacation in Vegas that it can entertain me endlessly.

In no time, we're pulling into the valet parking of what looks like the tallest building on this side of the Strip. Large, turquoise lettering spells out La Flor on the front. Giant red and pink neon flowers surround it. We step out onto gold carpeting and wait while Stone gives the valet driver a handshake.

"Let's check in." Antonio nudges me with his arm. I follow him through the glass revolving door, praying the whole time that I don't get stuck, before stepping into the elegantly decorated lobby. Gold marble covers every surface along with a bouquet of brightly colored flowers, not overly gaudy, but obviously expensive. The atmosphere exudes equal amounts of business and pleasure.

"He's looking for you," the icy looking receptionist warns before Antonio even gives her his card to check in with. His brown eyes roll almost behind his sockets.

"We just got here. We're early. We'll be down in fifteen," Toni states. The woman doesn't respond and quickly taps out a message on the smartphone next to her keyboard.

"He said ten," she replies before handing us four room keys.

Toni grabs my arm and leads me toward the elevators. "Can you go up on your own? We'll be up in a few minutes, we just have to take care of a few small things first."

"Roll call?" I asked curiously.

"Something like that." He laughs before handing me one of the keys.

"I don't know where I'm going," I remind him.

"Oh, shit," he responds, grabbing a Sharpie out of his backpack and writing on my room key. "Room 2666. Twenty-sixth floor at these elevators, go left then it will be the sixth door on your right."

"K," I tell him before hoisting my backpack up farther. "See you soon."

"Later." He waves before heading back to meet up with Stone and Joe.

Thankfully, no one else enters the elevator and I have a few minutes alone to breathe. Plucking my phone from my pocket, I stare at the three unanswered texts from Jay.

Jay: Did you girls make it okay?

Jay: Make sure you try the In And Out by campus. I swear it's the best one in the entire state.

Jay: Baby, give me something here. I'm kind of worried.

I sigh reading the last text. Lying to get out of town was one thing. Continuing the charade now that I'm not under his supervision feels like crossing a line we might not come back from.

Me: I miss you.

I tap out quickly while navigating down the long hallway. It's the truth and at least he'll know I'm alive. I nod to myself believing my justification trumps all the secret keeping he does.

Jay: I miss you too. Behave yourself :P

"Shit." I groan into the empty space. The door to the room looms in front of my face, yet it feels far away. Once I go in there, I'm really in deep with this plan of mine. Which means playing the role of Blake's little sister, following around the coolest guys and being in awe of *everything*.

The minute the door opens to the room I'm fully aware that I may have made a mistake. *I see you're running with the Baby-Face crew.* Trent's observation haunts me while I look around the very elaborate, very expensive suite. The main living area alone is larger than my whole apartment. Padding over to the crystal bar, I notice all the liquor is top shelf. The television on the farthest wall is almost the size of a movie theater screen and the smaller flight of stairs that leads to a separate sitting area before splitting off into three bedrooms and a bathroom is something out of a catalog. These are the rooms hotels usually use to set up the VIPs and the high rollers. Basically, the type of guests they want to keep happy and keep at their hotels and casinos. Not just three guys helping the workers who are hoping to make a little extra cash.

I type out a quick group text to see when they will be up. My stomach has a dull ache warning me I need food and soon. Stone replies instantly telling me to get room service and that they will be out for a while. Joe replies next, telling me to relax and enjoy myself. Toni chimes in last, letting me know that there are a few good movies on the TV and I can charge it to the room. Shrugging, I place an order with the kitchen before plopping down on the couch and flipping through the channels. Nostalgia floats around me in a protective bubble. Memories of every other time I would join the guys in Vegas plays out in my mind. My body attempts to relax while trying to ignore the reminders of how this time is also different.

When the food arrives, Stone, Joey, and Toni are still not back. I text them again letting them know the food arrived. Unlike the last time, they don't respond. I try making myself comfortable on the spacious couch while balancing my burger and fries on my lap and the beer from the mini-fridge next to me. Each crunch from my french fries echoes in my ears reminding me how alone I am. Did I make the right choice to come here? I could be at my house with Jay right now. Or actually at UNLV with Jenna and her friends checking out the campus and parties, acting like most eighteen-year-olds. After eating and my brain quiets down, I grab a blanket off one of the beds upstairs and decide to lay on the couch. If the guys come back, I'll hear them and can ask what they've been up to. Tucking my phone into the pocket of my hoodie, I try to concentrate on the rerun episode of *The Big Bang Theory*, the silence lulling me into sleep.

———

SUN FILTERS THROUGH the curtain in the room the next morning, pulling me out of a deep sleep. I sit up when I realize I'm still on the couch. A loud snore from upstairs. I frown, realizing I slept through them coming back and have no idea what they've been up to. Standing to my feet, I survey the room quickly. Nothing is out of place. The room service cart is gone and three pairs of shoes now lay by the door. Rubbing the sleep from my eyes, I shuffle to the bathroom to splash water on my face. On my way out, I run face-first into a warm slab of concrete flesh.

"Ow," I mutter, almost falling back on my heels.

"Whoa." Joe laughs, using his arms to steady me. "I called your name, but you were zoned out."

"Oh." I frown, rubbing my forehead. "I was just about to order breakfast, do you want anything?"

"No worries," Joe replies, smiling. "We're actually about to get ready and grab some food down by the poolside cabana. Work, ya know?" He shrugs.

"The pool?" I ask, not wanting to appear too excited. Relaxing by a pool sounds amazing right now.

"Mm-hmm," he replies while walking up the stairs before yelling over his shoulder. "Hurry up and get ready!"

I waste no time running to my backpack and grabbing my suit and cover-up. I run my hands through my hair and quickly pull it into a topknot on my head. I just finished slipping my flip-flops on when Joey and Stone head down the stairs. My jaw drops when I notice them dressed similarly in light jeans and button-up short sleeve shirts. Joey's hair is gelled and styled to perfection, he has a large silver watch placed on his wrist that screams expensive. Even Stone cleaned up, his bun slicked back, no unruly curls anywhere. He has all black Ray-Bans clutched loosely in his fingers.

"Did I miss the formal invitation?" I ask, raising my eyebrow at them. I am simultaneously freaked out because I've never seen them look this put together while at the same time overly curious as to why. Not to mention a small part of my heart skips a beat because they look mature and grown up and I should be happy for them.

"Yeah, yeah, smartass." Joey laughs. "Let's go." He signals for me to follow.

"What about Toni?" I ask just before another snore can be heard from upstairs.

"He was out, a little late last night," Stone answers while closing the room door behind me. "He'll be down later."

I let it go and follow them back down the hallway and to the elevators. By the time we reach the lobby and take an outside trail to where the pool is, my back had a light sheen of sweat from the hot temps. The surprises keep coming when the guys lead me to a private poolside cabana where we are instantly waited upon by a chick who clearly works out daily, and probably skips meals, in a bright neon turquoise swimsuit.

"Aren't you working?" I ask them while stuffing another bite of French toast into my mouth.

"Yes, Palmer," Stone answers, showing me a stack of cards. Leaning closer, I take one from him. The front is black and shiny. Gold lettering spells out Corazon with NightClub in English underneath. "These all need to get handed out today," he tells me. Nodding, I sit back in my chair. They get up and walk around the pool in shifts, sometimes disappearing from my view before coming back. When the food and mimosas are gone, I peel down to my swimsuit and lounge back in a partly sunny area. My phone still shows no new messages, so I tap a quick text to Jay telling him I'm having fun before grabbing my earbuds and playing my playlist and closing my eyes.

A shadow moves over me causing my eyes to fly open. Right away, I'm met with Toni's smirking expression and I can't help the sneer that moves over my lips. "What?" I ask, feeling annoyed at being woken up.

"Making up some extra z's today, Blaisey?" he inquires, the smile only getting bigger. "You were sawing logs when we got home last night and drooling all over the cabana recliner this afternoon."

"Was not," I reply defensively, touching my fingers to the corner of my mouth. All this does is earn a laugh that causes a small blush to tinge my cheeks.

"It's okay," Toni replies, shrugging before lifting his eyes to me. "T's a sexy look."

"Shut up," I tell him while sitting up in the chair. By now, the majority of the people have left the pool area. The sun is lower in the sky, close to creating that pinkish-orange glow.

"Guess I was really out of it," I mutter to myself while checking for signs of a good sunburn.

"Sure were, babe," Toni agrees. "I was sent to get you. The guys already went up to get ready for tonight."

"What's tonight?" I ask while sliding my cover-up over my head and locating my phone and shoes.

"Grand opening of La Flor's nightclub," he tells me. We fall into step next to each other as we head inside. "We'll be working there tonight, but at least you can enjoy it. It's crazy cool on the inside."

"I don't have anything to wear," I remind him.

"Already taken care of." He shrugs again like it's not a big deal. I grimace.

"No offense, I'm sure she's a nice girl, but I don't want to wear someone else's clothes when I don't know them. Especially not clubbing attire."

He laughs again, causing the people in the elevator to look at us sideways. "Nah nah nah, we had some stuff delivered from the store downstairs. You pick what you want and it gets charged to the room." He waves me off.

"Seriously?" I ask, completely dumbfounded. "This is like something out of a chick flick with a makeover scene. Shit like that never happens in real life."

He leans down to look straight in my eyes, his are lit up and slightly glazed. "Tonight, it's your real life, Blaisey. You deserve good things to happen to you," he says before turning and heading toward the room. I'm frozen watching his retreating back. Toni's words sink in my skin and fill a place inside my soul. I don't want to feel weak while I'm here, but there is something about these guys that brings out the urge in me to protect. I've known them the majority of my life. We were a family to each other when our home lives were a mess of epic proportions. Blake always said he would do anything for these guys and I can see why. Even as I think the thoughts, the twinge of betrayal in my chest is there. Stone, Toni, and Joey are family, but Jay has been steadily working his way into my heart. Guilty, I look down at my cell and realize it's dead.

"Great," I mumble to myself before trailing Toni to the door. Inside the room, two racks of clothes are lined up. One is filled with suits, designer jeans, and shirts for the guys. On the other, there is so much sparkle, I almost wince. Walking closer, I turn each item over one by one. To my relief, only the first three are obscenely short, sparkly, and colors I wouldn't be caught dead in. I'm not much of a color person to begin with. Black, white, and grey are the staple colors of any shirt, dress or hooded sweatshirt I own. My mom used to tell me to buy things in blue because it would accentuate my eye color. I stopped listening about the same time she also told me I better wear a padded bra or else boys wouldn't like me. I was twelve. Shaking the thoughts away, I reach for the nude material in front of me. Biting my lip, I take it into the bathroom, silently staring it down the entire time I shower, straighten my hair, and add a little mascara and lip gloss to my face. I can hear the guys out in the living room and I know my time is almost up. I step into the skirt and pull it up over my hips before sliding the halter straps around my neck. Surprisingly, the dress is not as short as I expected and the cut-outs around my waist are held together by more straps of the material. I turn my back to the mirror and do a little dip and bend. The motion doesn't cause my ass to be exposed and I breathe a sigh of relief.

Stepping out into the room, I'm met with wolf calls and whistles that make blood rush to my head. My cheeks burn and even my ears feel like they're on fire.

"Stop," I tell them, holding out my hand before flicking them my middle finger.

"You look all grown up, little Palmer," Joey tells me before pulling my body into a side hug. I glance at each of them and am taken aback by their appearance as well. Designer jeans fall and hug their legs perfectly. Only Toni's are styled and ripped to perfection. Joey's t-shirt molds perfectly to his lean chest and an open blazer hangs perfectly on his frame. Stone's black button-up tapers perfectly around his trim waist while hugging his muscular arms. They are a sight to see and will no doubt be gaining a lot of female attention tonight.

Rolling my eyes, I wrap my arm around Joey's waist and steer him toward the door. "Let's get going, Romeo." We make it right out the door when I stop suddenly.

"Shit, I forgot my phone." I hold out my hand for a room key.

"Where ya going to put it?" Toni snorts, eyes roaming up and down the tight-fitting dress. I frown, realizing he's right.

"Just leave it to charge." Stone lifts his shoulders, appearing bored with the situation. "You can text the boyfriend tomorrow that your phone died. I'm sure he'll live."

My frown deepens when I realize I forgot to text Jay at all today. I bite my lip hoping he isn't freaking out. "Yeah," I tell them. "I'll text him later." Hopefully, he'll buy the *I've been so busy touring the campus line.* Even thinking it causes goosebumps to race over my skin. My list of apologies grows longer and longer every day.

Corazon lives up to its name. The low red lighting in private booths, deep red velvet draping and neon heart signs give the allure that everyone was falling in love there tonight. It also helped that they had secured residency for one of the hottest DJs in the US. I was in awe of the elegance and expense the place was vibing. Thankfully, I was with people who knew what they were doing and where they were going. More so everyone else knew where we were going, judging by the way men and women stopped conversations just to turn and look at the guys. A few received fist bumps, head nods and, those lucky scandalously looking ladies received side hugs. I appeared invisible and I was grateful. Probably helped that the guys created a barrier between my body and prying eyes.

Stone led us to the biggest private booth in the back. A sheer red curtain came partially down from the ceiling and left only a foot of space from kissing the top of the leather seats. Candles littered the table in front of us. A bottle of top shelf vodka sat in an ice bucket open and ready.

"Drink?" Stone asks after we all sat down.

"Not yet, thanks," I reply while shaking my head.

"Be right back," Joey announces before heading across the dance floor toward what looked like a possible bachelor party.

"Does he know them?" I question since Joey never mentioned anyone else joining us.

"Working." Toni laughs over his cell phone that he's been on since we left the room. I nod, mulling over the discussion.

"You can go dance or get a drink if you want, little B. We'll be here," Toni adds and smiles wide.

The energy in the room has picked up as more bodies fill the space. Music blasting from the sound system creates a sensual and fun beat.

"Okay," I announce, standing. "I'm going to dance. I will hate myself if I don't." They laugh and watch as I make my way to the floor.

One song turns into three, which turns into a few shots from the bottle on the table and before I know it, sweat is dampening my hairline and my chest is soaked in warmth. The room has to be at max capacity by now, making the night a success for the grand opening. It does not escape my notice that almost everyone has made their way to our booth to talk to the guys at least once. I'm also not stupid enough to not have seen money being passed around like it's candy.

When the music slows, I make my way off the floor and over to the booth. The conversation stops until I have a new drink in my hand. The vodka cran goes down smooth, the chill chasing away the heat from my body.

Not until after the drink is gone do I realize everything is all wrong. The people in this booth are looking at me with hostility and I can sense that Joey appears more tense than normal. His jaw locks and his eyes harden at the guy across from him. I turn to him, wanting to ask what's wrong. My protective instincts from the good ol' days are kicking in, but my vision blurs. Blinking, I watch as Joe's face shifts in front of mine. My body feels sluggish and wants to shut down, to fall asleep, while my brain screams frantically for me to move away. Instinctively, I reach out for Joey but I miss his arm, the momentum sending me forward onto the seat and into blackness.

I knew it was a dream when I looked up and saw the picture of the six of us from our high school days sticking out of the visor. Blake kept it in there all the time. Which meant when I looked down and saw my hand gripped around the tan steering wheel of his cherry red Impala, it was confirmed I was out of it. That car was smashed and bent in odd places. Only now I was flying. My eyes widened while the speedometer kept creeping up. My heart hammered in my chest, my eyes stung with tears. Real fear, the kind that steals your breath and makes your body ache before the adrenaline kicks in, raced through my body. My foot pumped endlessly on the brake pedal, but I wasn't stopping. The tree I knew was coming grew closer and closer and the car only sped up.

"No!" I scream into my arms, throwing them up to shield my face, though the impact doesn't come. When my arms lower, I'm back in Corazon. The party continues, only no one notices me. My gaze shifts to the booth we were partying in. A dark form sprawled out on the seat. My feet pull me closer even though I don't want to see. I don't want to know what is happening. My breathing comes in deep and short, practically sucking the life right out of me. This is going to kill me.

My body stops at the edge and I'm forced to look. Confusion rolls through me when I realize I'm looking at myself. Asleep. Not broken or bloody or torn apart. My head tilts and scans the area, but I'm still invisible.

I feel him before I see him. His freshwater, citrus, and sandalwood scent sinks into my skin bringing with it peace and despair. He smells like home. Like my childhood. Like my protector. Like the pillow he slept on for thirteen years that I kept for months after he left me, crying into it every night. Hating myself when that smell went away because I knew I'd never have it again. Turning my head, I meet his eyes and my knees want to buckle. Blake has no scratches, no blood, the tone of his skin has the same sun-kissed tan. His eyes move over me from my head to my toes and up. When our gazes connect, I can read the sadness in his.

***I'm sorry**, his mouth moves, but the words don't come.*

Shaking my head. "Don't. It wasn't your fault. I miss you so much," *I tell him. My words break when a sob catches in my throat. His brow furrows, his eyes sliding from me to the sleeping form on the seat before returning back to me. His hands are suddenly gripping my arms, his face inches from mine. He looks panicked and scared, his mouth moving again. I concentrate on his lips and still can't hear anything. Blake's grip is painful, his fear transferring into my body until my pulse races, my mind becomes frantic. Blake never worried. He never let anything bother him. My body sways in his grip. Screeching tires and shattering glass sound around us, our bodies fall to the floor.*

Wake up, his voice is muffled, like I'm swimming underwater.

Wake up Blaise. My mind fights to listen, to hear, to see.

Wake up!

"The fuck," I hear Joey grit between his teeth. "How much?"

"You heard what Alverez said, he didn't want her lucid while Reyes was in the room," Toni responds.

"Yeah, so get her drunk not... Jesus, I can't even fucking say it," Joey growls at him.

My head is pounding, little fragments of the night coming back to me. Taking inventory of my body, I can tell I'm on something soft, probably the bed I hadn't used yet and my dress is still on and I'm covered with a blanket. I purposely keep my eyes closed, letting them think I'm still passed out. Names they keep repeating, Alverez, Reyes, Mamacita, names that mean nothing to me, yet somehow still seem important. Despite the splitting headache waiting for me once I open my eyes, I work to commit those names to memory. Hopefully, they'll mean something to Jay.

"Jay." His name comes out breathy from my throat, that I now realize feels like is packed with cotton balls. Two sets of eyes swing to me when I sit up. "Phone," I managed to croak out, keeping my eyes partially closed from the offensive light coming through the window. Fuck Vegas and its constant heat and sun right now.

"How ya feeling, champ?" Toni asks, nudging my bed with his foot.

"Yeah." Joey clears his throat before placing his fake smile on. "You partied hard last night, Blaisey."

"I quit counting her shots after they played Usher," Toni tells him, laughing at my expense.

"Phone," I say again, holding my hand out. "And water," I add. Joey laughs before leaving the room to get my requests.

"What happened?" I ask Toni once we're alone.

His head cocks to the side. "You passed out. We got you to the room. It's okay to relax a little, Blaise, everyone needs to sometimes."

I watch him intently looking for any sign of his conscience knowing he just lied to my face. Fragments from last night come back. I may have had a couple shots and a drink, but I knew my limit. I had not been at the point where I would have no memory of leaving Corazon, let alone, the walk to the hotel room.

Before I can voice this, Joey returns to the room. "Here," he says, not meeting my eyes. I flip the screen over.

74 Missed Calls

20 Texts Jay

5 Texts Jenna

"Shit!" I fly off the bed, unlocking my phone.

Jay: Are you okay? I tried calling earlier but it goes to voice.

Jay: Blaise. Seriously.

Jay: I stopped by Señor Locos. Jenna was working. Molly got sick and you all came back early. Only you didn't because you never were with them.

Jenna: I'm so sorry! I didn't know we were your alibi. :(

Jenna: Just call him. I'm sure he'll forgive you once you tell him what's up. :)

Jay: Where are you Blaise?

Jay: I'm pissed and fucking freaking out. WHERE THE FUCK ARE YOU?

Jay: Are you in Vegas?

Jay: Please don't tell me you were naïve enough to go to Vegas with them.

Jay: Baby, please answer me. I need you to tell me where you are.

Jenna: Where you at girl? Homeboy here is not looking too good.

Jenna: Seriously babe you're freaking us all out. :(:(:(

They go on and on. Two things for sure, I'm fucked and Jay knows I lied. Biting my bottom lip, I turn toward Toni. "I need to go now."

"We're leaving in one hour, Blaisey. Go shower and freshen up. We're almost ready," he tells me before they leave the room, closing the door behind them.

I don't wait. I bolt for the bathroom, shower, place my wet hair into braids and wash all the makeup from last night off my face. I don't feel sore or like I've been violated, yet I make sure to fully scan my body from head to toe anyway. No marks or bruises, except from Jay's mouth, are anywhere on me. Sighing in relief, I sink to the floor. The room spins when my eyes close and my stomach heaves. I only have seconds to make it to the toilet before everything I consumed in the past twenty-four hours makes its way out of my body.

Me: I'll be home soon.

I tap out my reply to Jay knowing it won't matter at all until I'm in front of him, and he can see me. I wait for the little dots to appear and frown when they don't.

"Fuck," I mutter to myself, letting my head rest against the side of the tub. Everything hurts. Tears slide down my face with the realization that I was drugged. There is no other explanation. Last I remember I was buzzed, no doubt, but I was not blackout passed-out drunk. My stomach recoils thinking that now I have to spend a car ride with Stone, Antonio, and Joey. I don't trust them. Someone did this and if it wasn't them, they know who did.

Using the sleeve of the t-shirt I threw on, I wipe my tears and proceed to brush my teeth all over again. We make it out of the room and into the car without a problem. The space is silent, no one talks or jokes. It's definitely not the carefree drive we had on our way there. I have many guesses why and choose to keep silent. I let my sunglasses fall down to my nose and watch through dark lenses while Toni counts the stacks of money from his pocket. And by stacks I mean stacks. Stacks of multicolored green, American bills. Twenties, fifties, hundreds. I watch as he finishes counting his then counts Joey's and Stone's in the same process. Nausea shifts my stomach again and I steel myself against it. I asked for this. I needed to see. I just didn't think it would leave such a sting in my heart. The saddest part about this betrayal is that it never comes from your enemies. It comes from those who already know your weaknesses and can exploit it for their own gain. Now I know how far they could go.

By the time we make it into town, the sun has set and the street lights are popping on. I flip my phone over again and still have no messages from Jay. Jenna did text me back and after giving me the third degree, she had settled down somewhat. I'm nervous to face him. Part of me wants to go to his place and the other wants to get to Señor Locos to see if he is there, too. Maybe if there's a crowd, he'd be less likely to murder me.

Stone drops me off first and I can't get out of there fast enough. "Thanks," I say and shoot them some deuces.

"You'll feel better tomorrow," Toni assures me, making me want to vomit all over again.

"Get some rest," Joey calls, shaking his head. I nod and walk backward to my door. Stone watches me before shifting to drive and taking off. Somehow, his silence unnerves me more.

Running up to my door, I unlock the row of locks before stepping inside. The room is pitch black until I find the light switch. The kitchen light instantly turns on. There is no note for me on the counter from my mom, not that I'm surprised, and the note I had left her is now in the garbage can next to the counter. I kick off my sandals before hiking my backpack on my shoulder and feeling my way down the hallway to my room.

Twelve

THE AIR CRACKLES WITH ENERGY AND heat before I even open my door. I know what I'm going to find. Sucking in a breath, I push the door open and step over the threshold, steeling my spine, ready for the battle ahead. Jay sits on the edge of my bed, his phone resting in his hands. His body is wound tight, his shoulders bunched under the red hoodie he's wearing. His eyes slowly rise to meet mine, scanning over my body, no doubt looking for the same injuries I had looked for this morning. When the deep brown orbs meet my blue ones, anger, fear, worry, and another emotion I'm not ready to name flash through his. Even knowing he's on edge, I refuse to budge. I acknowledge I didn't make the smartest decision and I was drugged, but I needed to do something. I'm not the girl that sits and waits for her boyfriend, if I can even call him that, to fix everything. If it's the last thing I ever do, I will find out what happened to my brother. A small dose of evil worked its way into my life this weekend. My eyes are now open to the demons hiding in plain sight. Not looking away, I lift my chin defiantly, matching the heat of his gaze, baiting the caveman lurking behind that beautiful face. Waiting for the storm of his fury.

"Ramirez asked me to meet him for lunch yesterday so we could catch up. When Jenna walked up to take our order, I knew something wasn't right," Jay states while his eyes bore quietly into mine. I want to look away while my body shifts from side to side. The pang of guilt hits my chest all over again.

"We both were this close to calling you in as a missing person." Jay holds his fingers up with just barely a bit of space between them. "Until some kid at the bar said you were with Stone, Antonio, and Joe." The way he says their names, there is no denying his hate for them. I bite my lip, knowing I've hurt Jay and probably gave Sarge a panic attack, too.

"I can explain if you let me," I try to reason, wanting to tell Jay my side, too.

"Did you go to Vegas with them?" he asks, interrupting. His jaw locked, his eyes cold and distant.

I move farther into my room, keeping my back straight and my head held high. I nod and watch his face contort into rage. "Jay—" I start to reason.

"You've got to be fucking kidding me!" Jay stands from my bed, raking his hands through the short sides of his hair. "After everything, everything we've talked about? After I told you that they're possibly dangerous and we promised to trust each other, you think that was the smart thing to do?"

"Stop!" I tell him, holding up my hands. "Listen to me. I can explain."

"What is there to fucking explain, Blaise?" His voice booms in the small space of my room. "You lied. There is no trust between us and you put yourself in a dangerous situation. How do I know you weren't giving them details of everything I've told you over the last month?"

"I wouldn't do that," I respond, recoiling that he thinks that low of me.

"Why should I believe you?" he answers, crossing his arms over his chest.

"Look, I'm sorry I lied. I knew the minute I decided to go we might end up here, but I couldn't just sit around either, Jay. This whole thing has been a nightmare for me, too. I'm being told one thing by one person and one thing by another. At this point, I don't know who to trust. I needed to see for myself if they've changed. I grew up with them. They aren't just strangers who moved to town when you got here. I trust you and then I felt guilty, so guilty that I gave up any allegiance to them. I condemned them just because you said so." I drive my point home by jabbing my finger into his chest.

Jay leans down so his face is level with mine. "Because I'm right, Blaise. You know it, I know it. I asked you to let me handle it so you wouldn't have to face the reality of what could happen."

"And I'm not some princess who needs you or anyone to do all the dirty work for me. I needed to know for me, Jay. I wish you could understand that." My voice cracks with emotions I've been storing for the past twelve hours.

"I wish I could, too. If you had told me, I could have tried. That's how relationships work," he answers, lifting his shoulders.

"Are we in a relationship?" I ask. "Because last I knew, you wanted to fuck whenever possible, but it's sort of pretend and it's sort of your job."

His eyes turn black and he shakes his head. "Unbelievable. Okay,

Blaise, keep going with that then. If that makes you feel less like a shitty person for what you did, then keep believing that shit you tell yourself."

"Fuck you," I spit out, an angry flush spreads across my cheeks. He's on me, my body pinned between the door and him before I even have the words out of my mouth. My first instinct is to struggle before my hands are locked above my head in his vise-like grip. We're both breathing heavily, fuming over our argument.

"You'd like that, wouldn't you princess," he replies, his lips dropping to the exposed flesh on my neck, using his tongue to draw a wet path up to my chin.

"Don't call me that," I warn him, attempting to bring my leg up and get some distance between us. Lust builds in my chest sending warmth through my body and a strong pulse between my legs. I want him even though I'm angry. I wanted him to be angry still.

"What does Mamacita mean?" I asked, my voice barely above a whisper. Jay's body becomes rigid, his face instantly pulls back, his eyes pin me with a glare.

"Where did you hear that?" His voice deathly serious while he moves back, dropping my hands like I burned him. "Blaise, where did you hear that?"

I look away, unable to meet his gaze knowing the next words out of my mouth are going to cause a whole new catastrophe between us.

"I saw Seth," I tell him, clearing my throat.

"The fuck, where?" Jay steps farther away from me, his hands tugging at the longer hair on top of his head.

"He came here," I answer quickly, my tongue darting out and running across my dry lips. I feel my pulse speeding up.

"When?" Jay asks.

"Before I left with the guys," I answer honestly. The truth is supposed to set you free but all I feel is more twisted in knots. Jay shuts down in front of me. A mask slides over his face, while his eyes look at me as if he doesn't know me.

"Where is he?" Jay's tone is icy at best while he detaches from all his emotions.

"I don't know." I shrug. "Honestly. He was just here, and he was freaked out and he has what you need but he doesn't know who to trust either. He told me to ask Trent about Mamacita. He said that—"

"Nichols knows about this?" he questions, anger flaring to life in his eyes again.

"What? No. I never asked him. I wanted to ask you when I got back, but I kept hearing it in Vegas and I—"

"Stop," Jay says, holding up his hands. "Was she there?"

"Who?" I ask, confused. My brain spins trying to remember if any women were with us when they referred to Mamacita. "No, I don't think so."

"You don't think so," Jay repeats, his head cocked to the side. I hate the sneering look on his face while he stares at me. "Of course not."

"Maybe if everyone was honest with me and quit using codes and games all the time, I wouldn't be trying to figure this out on my own. I wouldn't be taken back and would know who I should be looking out for!" I practically scream at him. All my previous frustrations are back with a vengeance.

"And, if you had been honest with me, this could have been something we talked about. I have to go report in," Jay tells me, sliding past me to get out of my bedroom door. I listen as he stomps down the hallway and jump when he slams the door shut before the lock slides into place.

Everything comes crashing down on me at once. My legs buckle and my chest heaves while sobs rock my frame. I'm overwhelmed and way out of my depth. Mourning the relationship with the boys I used to know, who used to sneak me Cheetos in my lunch, would pick me up from school if Blake couldn't, and who never failed to give the best gag-gift Christmas presents, is still fresh. Jay's anger, even if I deserved it, stings the worst out of all the pain I'm feeling. Despite my best intentions, okay, my own stubbornness to find answers, I'm no better off than I was before. All I know is that I've been betrayed. We were betrayed.

Pulling myself to my feet, I trudge down the hall, standing in front of the closed door. Breathing in and out before bringing my hand to twist the knob. It's been months since I last opened his room and I'm terrified of the ghosts lurking inside. The door creaks initially, the sound echoing in the empty apartment, before it swings completely open.

"What the hell?!" I snap at Seth right as he climbs through Blake's window.

"Blaise?" he stammers, guilt flashing in his eyes.

"What are you doing?" I ask, rushing at him and tugging his hoodie so he tumbles to the ground.

Rolling to his back, Seth holds his hands up in defeat. "Wait! I'm sorry, I didn't mean to scare you."

"Doesn't answer my question," I yell at him, trying to remember where I left my phone and calculating how fast I could get there.

As if sensing my thoughts, Seth reaches out, his arm snaking around my ankle. "Wait, just listen. I have the money that McCall is looking for, okay. Blake gave me the bag and he took the other bag of evidence before he died."

"Where is it?" I ask, my brow furrowing.

"The money is safe. I will give it to you or McCall or whoever. I can't give the evidence though. That's what I'm trying to look for. I know how bad this looks, trust me, I get it. I have what everyone is after but the big guns… I don't know where your brother hid it." His words rush out of him. I lift my brow.

"Where's the money?" I asked, noticing the backpack he had last time isn't present.

"Not on me at this second. It would have been hard scaling up here if I had it, but I do have it," he assures me while climbing up off the floor.

"It's not in here," I lie, sweeping my hand around the room. "I went through everything, there isn't anything in here."

Seth studies me. "Are you sure? Under the bed, everything?"

"Yes!" I yell in a whisper, angry that once again Seth has just shown up. "I would know. Now get the hell out."

Anger flares in my stomach, and I begin shoving him back toward the window.

"Blaise, please." Seth's hands come out in front of him, clasped together. "Please believe me. I have the money. I didn't take it and split. I wouldn't do that. I don't trust anyone but you."

Our eyes connect and all the old feelings come rushing in again. The very first time I met Seth, I swore up and down he was going to be our best friend for life. His green irises screamed honesty. Like us, Seth had been dealt a shitty hand in parents, yet he grew up to be respectful, smart, and to a certain degree, kind. He was standoffish and often gave the system the finger then turn around and he would carry groceries to the car for elderly women. My heart squeezes in response to him. I don't want him to trust me. I don't want to trust him anymore. A year ago, this wouldn't even be up for discussion.

"Everything's changed," I say even while my head rejects the words.

Seth swallows visibly. "Not everything, Blaise. I still care about you. It's been hell not being able to be here with you. I miss him so much. Blake would know what to do and I just don't." His shoulders slump. Seth looks like the weight of the world has been riding on him and my twisted heart can't find it in myself to comfort him.

"Please leave, Seth." My words sound as hollow as I feel. Everything is dead on the inside. If I shut down the feelings, I might be able to coast through this tangle of lies.

He doesn't answer me, but I know I hurt his feelings. Seth moves quietly to the window and climbs through, back down the fire escape. I wait in the dark until I hear his feet hit the dirt below and take off running. Moving to the window, I slam it shut and lock it before sliding Blake's old collector's baseball bat on top to keep it closed. Goosebumps break out over my flesh, the hair on my neck tingling and I back up without disturbing anything else.

Back in my own space, I pull my phone out, staring at the empty screen. No missed calls or texts. My heart lurches once before I shut it down. I will not be a pawn and I will not continue catching feelings. This case that I walked into willingly is causing havoc in my life. Before I can stop myself, I text a quick message to Luis that I'm sick and need a few days off, then power off my phone. I make sure my window is locked and pad throughout the apartment, checking the windows, and double checking the front door before also locking myself in my room. Flipping on the fan, I strip down before sliding under my covers. The blood roaring in my ears subsides and I can concentrate on breathing in and out. My body is as exhausted as my mind and before I know it, everything goes black and quiet.

Thirteen

Seventy-two hours. I gave myself three full days to wallow in the past and face the mistakes I made. After twenty-four hours, I caved and turned my phone on only to be disappointed. There was nothing from Jay. Only a text from Luis that my time off was approved, but he would need me back by Friday's dinner shift and after the high school football game ended. It was Thursday, I texted him to let him know I was coming in.

By the time I finally showered and got dressed, it's close to the dinner rush. Not caring if I'm on the schedule or not, I show up and don't miss the hint of relief on Luis' face when I get behind the bar so that he doesn't have to be.

"Sorry," I mumble to him, which only earns me a grunt in response.

After three hours, my body falls back into muscle memory and it feels good to be out doing something. For the most part, I ignore the chatter around me. It's when the door flies open and Antonio howls into the air and the room explodes in laughter and cheers that I finally snap out of it. I basically fell off the face of the earth for three days and not one of them sent a text or called. I keep my eyes averted while they find their booth and the crowd gravitates toward them.

"Must be a good night planned at the track," Jenna says, leaning over the bar. She says it quietly enough only for me to hear. I shrug in response. "Are you okay?" she asks me, this time her voice was laced with concern.

"Talk a minute?" I ask, nodding toward the back door.

"I'll drop these off then meet you out there." Jenna smiles mischievously before taking her drinks away.

I wipe my hands and head out toward the back, grabbing a loose cigarette from Luis on the way.

"Hey," he starts to say but can't argue. Two minutes later, Jenna joins me with a cigarette clasped in her fingers, too.

Unlike her, I don't light mine, just hold it at my side while we talk. "I'm sorry," I tell her. Since arriving tonight, I've been chewing the words around in my mouth knowing they aren't enough and that I can't give her more. Jenna huffs next to me.

"You should have told me." Her eyes bore into mine. "I wouldn't have asked questions and it sure as hell would have saved everyone a lot of worry."

I nod, knowing she's right. "I should have," I agree with her even though I'm unwilling to share at this point. Maybe Trent was right all along and it's better to not trust anyone.

"He was pretty upset," Jenna tells me, her eyebrow quirked. "I thought he was going to pummel Luis for not asking why you needed the weekend off."

I shake my head picturing it. "I'll apologize to him, too. None of that should have happened."

"You know why though, right?" Jenna asks. Our eyes meet again, mine apprehensive. I shrug. "He cares about your crazy ass. We all do. He kept saying you could be in danger." Crossing her arms over her chest, Jenna looks away.

"I know," I reply, keeping my face masked.

"I don't know what's going on, but I know when something isn't right. Ever since they've been back… things haven't been right."

I nod again. "I really am sorry."

A ghost of a smile crosses her lips. Dropping the half-smoked cig to the ground, Jenna heads to the door. "I forgive you," she says over her shoulder without turning around. Stunned, I turn to ask her why, why forgive me when I haven't been the greatest friend in the world, but she's already disappeared back inside. Dragging in a deep breath, I attempt to refocus my mind.

We were only gone for five minutes and yet the place is already busier than when I left. I'm behind on tab orders and need to work quickly before the servers' tables get too rowdy. The work keeps me busy the rest of the night. By the time it's last call, I realize Stone, Joey, and Antonio ate and left without a word to me. Chills chase down my back after a quick glance at my phone shows they didn't text either. We went hours without acknowledging each other, which only fuels my curiosity… what are they hiding?

The door chimes one more time, and my heart races, only to be disappointed as a man and woman enter, clearly on a date. Jay did not show up tonight like he usually would. The traitorous organ inside my chest squeezes. No text, no call, and it's been three days. I swallow past the lump of emotion caught in my throat.

"Cash register is set," I mutter to Luis while untying my apron strings.

"Heading out?" Luis asks, giving me the side-eye.

It takes effort not to roll my eyes back at him. "Yup," I answer with as little attitude as I can manage. He did just give me three days off. My shift is over though and all he has to do is close down. I cleaned, the glasses are in the washer, and money is accounted for. "See you tomorrow." I fling over my shoulder before hightailing it out the door. The minute I breathe in the dusty air, I can feel eyes on me. I shiver in response, keeping my head down and my bag pulled tight against my body until I get to my car. Slamming my keys into the ignition, the headlights sweep the darkness before I peel out of there.

"It's just your imagination," I try to reason with myself during the drive back to the apartment. My phone starts going off, the vibrations almost painful from where I have the phone squeezed between my thighs. I count five text messages by the time I pull into the lot.

Once I'm in park, I pick up the cell, hating that my fingers are shaking.

Seth: Meet me after your shift. I have something to show you.

Seth: Everyone will be at Scar tonight. It's safe

Seth: Have you been to McCall's loft yet?

Seth: Didn't think so. Meet me tonight. He rents above the mechanic shop.

Seth: Trust me. You need to see.

Me: What if I have been there?

I type out quick, holding my breath that I don't have to wait. The little dancing bubbles are instant.

Seth: If you had, you wouldn't be sleeping with him.

My jaw clenches and my cheeks turn pink. I never told Seth we were sleeping together. I remember he made the same comment before, and I shut it down. I lied the other night to him about Blake's room. I haven't been through it in months. For all I know he did put something in there. Which also means that window has been unlocked for a long time, too. My stomach swoops just thinking about it. Grabbing my bag and keys, I jog to the door and let myself in before locking every bolt in place behind me.

The room is quiet, more than normal, and eeriness I'm not used to fills the void space. Blindly, my hand searches for the light switch, hitting all the buttons once I find it. The room flooded with light causing my eyes to squint. A single piece of pink paper sits on the countertop next to a yellow receipt.

> Blaise—
> The lease is paid for up till next month. That gives you the time you'll need to make new arrangements. I'm leaving today. I need this time to work on myself. Feel free to get rid of whatever you don't want to keep.
> Sorry.
> Mom

Bile coats my throat as I swallow repeatedly, keeping the emotional vomit locked down. What kind of mother does that to their child? All my life, she's kept us at an arm's length, never putting us before herself. The only reason I made it to adulthood without being in the system was because of my brother. Sobs start to escape before I slap a hand across my mouth to hold it in. My eyes dart around, noticing for the first time the missing picture frames, DVD pile, and the afghan blanket that used to sit on the couch. Zero to sixty, anger that I've never felt before courses through my body. Stomping down to her room, I fling the door open. The bed is bare, the closet door is open and empty, as well. She actually freaking left.

She left me like I meant nothing to her. I'm just the child she created and then abandoned.

Tears sting my eyes, moisture catches on my cheeks before making my way to my room. Everything remains untouched. Full-on crying, I slip my cell from my pocket and bring up Jay's name.

Me: Can you come over please?

Nothing happens. Squeezing my eyes closed tighter, I give myself a little more.

Me: She left, Jay. She took her things and left me. Idk what to do.

Sliding down the door, I lay the phone out in front of me before pulling my legs to my chest. I let go. Everything I've been holding onto for the past week is cried into the bare skin on my arms. My body shakes from convulsing and my cheeks are sore from continuously wiping them. It's ugly and lonely, and helluva therapeutic. My head throbs by the time I glance at my phone again.

0 Messages

0 Missed Calls

Picking myself up, something I've been getting better at the past half a year, I make it to my bed before collapsing again. My chest heaves and rattles with the last few fragments of my emotional breakdown. Making a deal with myself, I decide to call instead.

"This mailbox is currently full..." Straight to voicemail. A new determination settles in my veins and I'm up off my bed before I give myself the chance to think it through. Reckless, yes. I am only eighteen. Throwing on a pair of black leggings and a black Raiders zip-up, I tie my hair in a loose braid before shoving my feet in my running shoes. Remembering the feeling of being watched earlier, I decide to take a page from everyone else's book and slide my window open. It's a small fall to the balcony below, then from there a big stretch to shimmy down the fire escape. Blowing out a breath, I swing my legs out the window and over the edge. My body slides down the side and I let go before I can talk myself out of it.

My feet hit the ground without any accidents. I say a quick thank you to Blake before reaching the shadows. Thankfully, the streetlight is out tonight and makes it easier to move. Rowland's mechanic shop is dark and closed. I search the windows at the top of the building where the loft is located. Seth's messages earlier irked me knowing he was right. I haven't been up there. Never has Jay even offered for me to come over. We usually split time between Señor Locos and my apartment.

"Hey," his voice whispers next to my ear at the same time Seth's hand lands on my shoulder.

"The fuck!" I whisper-yell at him, looking around to make sure we weren't heard. We both wait a few seconds before talking.

"I told you no one was around. There was a huge race at Scar tonight." Seth shrugs.

"How did you know I was here, I didn't text you back," I ask, feeling overly suspicious and leery right now.

"I've known you for how long now, Blaise," he replies, dragging his eyes up to Jay's window. I scoff.

"You think I don't know the suspense would eat you alive." He chuckles and I frown.

"Whatever," I mumble. "Let's just get up there."

"Right," Seth says, holding back a grin. "Wait up. I'll be back." He disappears around the back of the building. My neck cranes up, again contemplating how we're going to get in. Even if I stood on Seth's shoulders, we aren't tall enough. The loft is above the vaulted ceiling of the garage.

In true Seth fashion, he answers my thoughts without speaking.

A long black rope comes flying down the side and stops right next to the window. My phone vibrates in my pocket.

Seth: Go around back and use the fire escape to get to the roof.

Roof. My heart plummets just thinking about it. Sticking close to the building to avoid the cameras and motion lights, I finally make it to the fire escape. The climb up the ladder proves much easier than I anticipated. Seth waits for me by the ledge where we plan to hang down from. The rope is fastened to a hook that is locked against the wall.

"I'll go first." He nods before easing his body over the edge. At least it isn't a far drop to the window from where I'm standing. His knife cuts through the edge of the screen, and I hear a beeping noise before the audible sound of a lock gives way. "I don't even want to know," I whisper to myself. Seth's body disappears inside. Holding my breath, it seems forever before Seth's head pops out meeting my gaze, a grim mask on his face. He waves me down. While my body is in shape from running, I very much lack upper body strength. My arms and shoulders ache by the time I shimmy into the window. I rub my palms against my leggings trying to soothe the rope burn.

"Ready?" Seth asks, standing in front of me, keeping my vision shielded from the room.

I nod. Slowly, Seth steps away from me until he's back to my side. My vision tilts while the blood leaves my face. "That's me."

"I know." Seth's voice sounds like he's in pain. Only his pain can't compare to what I'm feeling.

I'm everywhere in this room. Large pictures, small pictures, candid pictures, posed pictures, my freaking high school yearbook picture. I'm laughing, talking, reading, running, working, and sleeping. Not an inch of wall is open. I walk over to the single desk against the other window in the room, the one that is on the front of the building, the one that faces my room. A very large, very expensive Nikon camera sits on top. A long tube sits next to it. I swallow.

"He's been watching me," I choke the words out. A plan of my apartment and the old high school sit on top of the desk. Stars located in various rooms where I spent time. Next to that is a framed picture of Blake, Trent, and Jay. A file with my mom and dad's name is next to that and a picture of me blowing out my sixteenth birthday candles on top.

"I knew it," Seth says, releasing a sigh. "I didn't know it was to this extent though."

"What do you mean you knew?" I ask, turning to face him. My guard comes flying back up. Jays voice echoes in my memories, *Blake ended up almost here, he was dead and a bag of money went missing along with your friend.*

"When Blake pulled me in, I wasn't fully on board with McCall and Nichols. They just didn't seem right. I get Nichols more now, he's seen and been around some fucked up shit… McCall though just always rubbed me the wrong way. Like he was mad at me about something. That night…" His voice drifts off, his eyes haunted "That night Jay wasn't in Vegas—"

"I know this already," I interrupt.

"No." Seth shakes his head. "Blake and McCall got into it a few days before everything was supposed to go down. About you. Blake said we'd talk after Vegas, but I heard your name a few times. At the last minute, Blake texted me that he had a bad feeling. We changed direction. Blake made that decision. He handed me the bag and said we'd meet up. He said McCall was already here and would meet up with us."

"He was here, like in town that night?" I ask, feeling confused. My mind spinning in different directions.

"That's what Nichols said. Said Blake knew too, and that's why we split and headed this way," Seth explains. All his words are jumbled. My brain can see the puzzle, yet I can't make the pieces fit. "I need to leave," I tell him, grabbing a few of the pictures off the wall and the framed one from the desk. At this point, I don't care if Jay finds out. I want him to know that I know he's been spying on me. Keeping tabs on me, and from the looks of it for a few years.

We have no idea what happened. There was a solid plan in place. We walked through every detail many times and we designated which hotel everything would go down at. I wasn't going to be in Vegas with them that night. I was doing surveillance on another piece of important detail in case things did go bad. The whole plan was flawless. Somehow though Blake ended up almost here, he was dead and a bag of money went missing along with your friend.

Fragments of conversation float in and out, wreaking havoc on my heart. Why are Seth and Trent on good terms? Did Jay lie? Or is Seth lying?

"Do you want me to come with you?" Seth asks, at least he has the decency to look guilty. He literally just shattered the rest of any normalcy I had.

I shake my head. "No. I need to be alone."

"You should contact Nichols. Go see him at Scar," his voice says behind me. I don't give him a response before making my way to the window. I waste zero time, grabbing the rope and using it to propel my way down to the ground. Screw climbing and Seth can go to hell to if he thinks I'm sticking around to help him.

Lies and more lies everywhere. Everyone is lying. Everyone has their own agenda and somehow I've been thrust into the middle of it. Why though? I know absolutely nothing. Blake kept me very secluded from his secret life. He also started to exclude me with his extracurricular activities in Vegas. He was a protector. He didn't use me to further himself or trust me with all his secrets if he would have thought for one minute I would be hurt by it. These people have overly underestimated my brother.

I jog across the street, zero fucks given if I'm seen now. I want to be seen. I hope this is caught on whatever fancy device Jay has been watching me on. If the guys have some secret surveillance on me now, too, good, bring it. Loudly, I climb up the fire escape onto the balcony before jumping up to my window. I don't even try to disguise that I'm sneaking in. My shoes scrape against the roughened siding, a small grunt leaves my mouth while I haul myself through the opening. Once I'm in, I let the glass fall back into place before locking it with a flourish.

"Take that, fuckers!" I shout into my room, shit, into the apartment because let's face it, the place is all mine now.

"Hanging out with Baird now?" Jay's voice floods my ears, sending adrenaline pumping throughout my body. I'm caught between wanting to run and being too scared to move. He would catch me anyway and easily.

Slowly, I turn my back to the window. Jay's tall frame is rigid against my closed door. He looks wound up and ready to pounce as if he can hear the stream of words in my head. Everything I got is telling me to run. Even if I were to try and throw myself out the window now, I wouldn't make it. Closing my eyes, I swallow down the defeat before pulling out the pictures I'd stolen.

"He showed me something interesting," I tell him, laying it all out on my bed. Jay's face stays impassive. "How long have you been watching me, Jay?" I ask, the burning need to know flares alive in my gut.

Without missing a beat, Jay's chocolaty orbs swing to mine.

"Seven hundred and twenty-eight days, fifteen hours and five minutes."

My mouth goes dry.

"You aren't even going to deny it?" I ask, watching him, looking for any sign that he might crack.

He shrugs. "I want those back," he demands, nodding his head toward the pictures littered all over my bed.

"No," I tell him, lifting my chin defiantly. "Why? Why do you have these?" I can't stop the tears gathering on my lashes. I don't want to break in front of him though.

"Why are you hanging out with Baird?" Jay repeats, pushing his body off my door, stalking toward me.

"He's the only one helping me and not treating me like I can't handle the truth," I respond, refusing to back down.

"Is he?" Jay's head tips back, laughing. "You don't need help, Blaise. You've been dealing with all of this head-on for months and you've handled it. Don't feed his ego that he's helping you."

"Fine. He's not lying to me at least." I shrug, feeling weary.

"Or, he's telling you his version of the truth," Jay states, his head tipping to the side. He's studying me intently. "Guess I underestimated my worth, my mistake."

"No, your mistake was underestimating mine," I answer. Little does he know I've wondered the same thing. My heart leans toward Jay while my mind fights to believe the person I've known the majority of my life. "Tell me your version then." The words come out even while my mind screams, *No*.

He chuckles. "Are you sure you want to go down that path, Blaise? Once you do, there's no going back."

I shrug. "I'll take my chances."

The silence in the room stretches between us, wound tight, ready to snap at any given moment. I'm prepared for Jay's dark secret, prepared to hear mortifying information about my brother. What I don't expect is the next words out of Jay's mouth.

"I've been in love with you since Blake first asked me to watch you."

I swear my heart stops at the same time my stomach drops. I swing my gaze back to Jay, who hasn't taken his from me. "I don't understand," I say, my tongue darting out to my dry lips. My whole mouth suddenly feeling like I swallowed cotton balls.

"When Blake first came on, I told you, it was small stuff. Whatever happened between him and the others on that trip to Vegas freaked the shit out of him. He wanted nothing to do with it. He started working with Trent and myself. Just information, identifying names to the faces we picked up on surveillance. When it became obvious we were focusing on the cartel... I made the decision to start surveillance on Blake's family. If anyone found out what he was doing, they would go after the family, as well. Blake was on board with this when I explained what we were dealing with. He couldn't care less about his mom. Only the most important person to him, he wanted watched twenty-four-seven."

"Me," I acknowledge, more tears gathering, hearing about my brother. "Guess you took the surveillance a little too far though, huh?"

"You were wearing dark purple jeans, a black sweater, and those." He points at my combat boots under the bed. "You didn't even see me. You walked past, laughing with that blonde friend of yours." Jay's voice comes out strained. "I agonized for months over the feelings I was getting every time it was my turn to watch you. I told Trent, and he told me to come clean to Blake. He wasn't too happy about it." Jay shrugs, a guilty smile full of trouble passes his lips.

"I bet," I scoff.

"We agreed to talk about it after the case," Jay interrupts before I can say more. "Things were tense when it came to you, I took myself off your surveillance team to help."

"Where were you the night my brother was killed, Jay?" I beg the question threatening to tear me apart.

"I should have been there." His gaze leaves me for the first time, remorse slashing on his face. "Blake called me that morning and said something was off. He begged me to come here and watch you, because they'd find you. So I did. You went to school, came home, did homework, talked to your friends on Facebook, and then went to bed. He called me once and that was the last I heard until the news of the accident came through the radios."

"If you had been there, would things have been different?" My voice cracks through my tears.

Jay's eyes hold mine. Without saying a word, I know it wouldn't have. They both would have wanted to be here regardless.

"So this whole time, you knew who I was," I repeat back what I've just heard. "You knew who I was the day of the funeral too, didn't you?" I ask, even though I know the answer. Jay's nostrils flare, his face flushing in anger. Not a hint of denial escapes his mouth. Fury swirls in my gut. I feel mislead, lied to, and exposed.

"Did you like knowing you were fucking a minor that day? Do you get off on that shit, Jay?" The words spew from my mouth, laced in acid. I want them to cut like barbed wire across his soul.

"It was your eighteenth birthday," he reminds me, calmly, barely reacting to the bait I'm throwing and it pisses me off more.

"Screw you, Jay." My lip curls. "You think you love me? You stalked me. You don't know me!"

He's on me before I can blink or I can finish giving him all my anger. I can't contain it anymore. Unfortunately for him, he's about to be collateral damage in my emotional tornado. He grabs for me right as I push at him, causing us both to lose balance and fall onto my bed. The pictures scatter while my mattress slams against the wall. Jay fights for dominance while I claw my way into his skin, hurling my body into his. I won't beat Jay in strength. I go for the jugular, literally biting, and spitting sharp words instead.

"It's all your fault. You should have known better. You liar." The heat from Jay's body rolls off onto mine when he finally pins my back to the bed. My legs instantly circle his waist to throw him off until he gets my hands above my head in a tight grip. His muscled arms strain against the material of his shirt, my own is starting to stick to my skin.

"Get off," I grit out, my teeth clashing when he smirks.

"Keep fighting me, baby," he growls into the sensitive skin on my neck. My body instantly shivers, a fierce need for Jay spreads from my toes to the roots of my hair. I should be disgusted, yet the dull ache between my legs is anything but. I'm aroused. I want Jay to take his aggression out on my body.

I turn my head to the side, hoping he can't see the need in my eyes. "I hate yo—" Jay swallows my words with his mouth, his tongue reaching in, and pushing them back down my throat.

He kisses me until my head spins and my lips are bruised. He's savage with my body, yanking the leggings down my legs while shoving the material of my hoodie up to my chin. Need, lust, and anger swirling together inside my chest, I waste no time in grabbing the edge of his jeans and shoving them down with his boxers until his long, thick cock springs free. My nerves are on edge when he pins his dark eyes on me. I wet my lips, enjoying the way his pupils dilate, following the motion of my tongue. His face hardens before he rips the thin fabric of my thong, tearing the material from my body. A cool breeze whispers across my bare pussy, my legs turn to jello and a rush of warmth gushes in my core.

Before I can breathe again, he slams his cock into me, filling me to the hilt. His body shoves mine across the bed, taking my sheets and blankets with us. My foot is caught in my leggings and the material of his jeans rub the insides of my thighs raw and I love it. Jay takes my mouth in a hot-searing kiss. He keeps one of my hands locked above us while my free hand grips the top of his hair, trapping it between my fingers. Animalistic noises are ripped from deep within his chest. My moans are in unison to the glide and thrust of his body into mine.

My body thrashes against his, chasing the brewing orgasm inside my core. I grip my legs tighter around Jay forcing his pelvic bone to hit the sensitive bundle of nerves building my climax. His long fingers pinch and pull at my nipples through the lacy material of the bra I'm still wearing because neither of us bothered to take it off.

"Oh god, Jay." My voice is hoarse, and I stroke my tongue across the shell of his ear. His body speeds up, his lips coast up my throat, biting, sucking, and leaving a hot path of moisture on their way back up to my lips.

"Fuck, you feel so good," he tells me between pulls of my lips. "How badly do you want to come on my cock?"

"Please, Jay," I beg, not caring, I just want what he can give me. Twisting my hips, bucking against him, I plead with my devil above me. "Please make me come."

My words hang in the air for two more thrusts of Jay's hips before he roars to life, dipping his hand between our bodies, stroking and pinching the bundle of flesh. When my climax hits, it's enough to buckle my body and force a lust-filled cry from my swollen lips. I barely come down before Jay pulls out of me, leaving a trail of fluids between my thighs. Without speaking, his eyes cut to mine, holding me hostage in his angry gaze. He slides his jeans up and fixes his long t-shirt before grabbing the baseball hat off the floor. Wordlessly, he slides his shoes back on before flinging open my bedroom door and stalking down the hallway.

My body shakes with emotion as I pull myself into a sitting position on the bed. I frantically sprint out of my bedroom after him. "Jay!" I call right as he disappears out the door, slamming it so hard the locks rattle.

A new round of sobs escape me and my knees threaten to buckle. I can only take so much and I've really reached my breaking point. I said hurtful words to Jay that I can't take back. On the other hand, he also betrayed my trust and lied to me since the day he first stopped into Señor Locos.

I want to be on his side.

I want him to look after me.

I want to trust him unconditionally.

Jay evokes a side of me I thought had died. The ability to feel and to be hopeful. I don't know if I love him. I sure as hell crave him, want him, and even enjoy his caveman tendencies and aggression. My heart hammers in my chest, aching for what we could have if we could just get our shit together and stop the lies.

Bone tired and weak, I force myself to relock the doors before shuffling to the bathroom. I'm unable to stop the silent tears and I seek comfort from their burning path down my heated cheeks to the open bites on my lips. My icy blue eyes connect with the girl in the mirror. She looks broken except for the flush in her cheeks and chest, proving she can come back to life. I slip under the steaming hot water, soaking the tension from my sore muscles. I stay there until the stream starts to cool. Wrapping my body into the biggest towel I own, I finally step back into my room. I sigh before throwing back the covers, not bothering to clear the clutter from the floor, and slide between my sheets. Jay's scent lingers in the fabric around me, lulling me into the sleep my body demands.

Fourteen

"WHERE DID YOU HEAR THAT?" Trent's voice turns icy, his impressive frame frozen. I watch his lips inhale and exhale a cloud of smoke into the chilled air. After the other night and at Seth's urging, I sought him out at Scar. Sneaking onto the land had been more of a challenge than anything. Trent rarely, if ever, made an appearance during the races. Now I knew he preferred to watch the action from above, presiding like a king over his subjects from the Look Out.

Trent didn't look surprised to see me. If anything, he acted like he was expecting me all night. I wondered briefly if Seth told him to look out for me or if Trent had talked to Jay.

"Which name?" I scoff, wrapping my arms around my waist, "They seemed pretty interchangeable. Toni was really freaked out though when they were discussing Alverez and Reyes."

"What about the other one?" he inquires, still unmoving from this spot. Trent's gaze is unfocused, zoned out while gazing at the dancing flames from the bonfire below.

"Mamacita?" I question, almost missing the slight flicker in his gaze. "That name seemed to be more used in regards to the club, like they were waiting for her or wanted her to be there," I answer, biting the inside of my cheek. I wracked my memories all morning trying to remember each and every detail that wasn't blurry from the car ride there to the car ride home.

"Did you see her?" he asks, taking a long drag in before throwing the still burning bud to the ground.

"No," I answer automatically. Even being drugged, I would have known if I'd seen her. The way the guys acted, it was as if she was the golden ticket. Trent is silent again, his forehead creased in thought. He slides an older model phone from his jacket, hitting the button once.

"Raul Alverez has resurfaced in Sin City," Trent relays into the phone. His tone is laced with boredom yet his posture is wound tight. I tilt my head, observing him. Trent's outer exterior screams danger, his movement mirrors those of a predator, and still his eyes laugh when they connect with mine. He knows I was sizing him up and I don't bother hiding it. Fewer surprises, the better.

"No." He smiles, almost chuckling. "I got eyes on her. Relax," he says. My pulse speeds up when I hear Jay's deep voice on the other line. I miss what he says and their conversation is quick, less than half a minute altogether.

"Causing trouble again, Palmer?" Trent grins, shaking his head. "I don't know who's worse sometimes."

Ignoring that comment, I roll my eyes. A comfortable silence stretches between us while we're both lost in thought. Gathering my courage, I confide in Trent the last piece of information I have to give. "I think I was drugged."

His face turns toward me, his eyebrows raise in question. "Think?"

"No." I shake my head slowly. "I was. I had a buzz, but not enough to make me blackout like that. I had dreams…" Sighing, I turn and catch his ocean blues with my icy ones. "When I woke up, Toni and Joey were talking about it. Well, arguing about it. That's when they started talking about Alverez and how he was telling him to make sure I wouldn't remember anything. Also, how Reyes wouldn't be happy and that their deal largely relied on that person."

"What do you remember last?" He turns to me, eyes piercing.

"I was dancing. I went back to the booth and took a sip of a new drink, then everything went dark." My voice comes out hollow. I've replayed the events in my head over and over again. There is something about saying the words out loud about what happened to me that makes it more real.

"Who was there?" he questions, finally sounding like the undercover cop he is.

"Men mostly, a few women. Like arm candy women. They looked higher than kites, pupils were huge, and they were extremely clingy." I say the word, puckering my face as if I ate something sour.

"Does Jay know?" Trent asks, lighting up a new cigarette.

"We're not really speaking," I answer truthfully, shrugging my shoulders.

"No shit," Trent replies sarcastically. I flip my middle finger at him which only earns me a harsh laugh. "Seth told you then, huh?"

"He showed me," I acknowledge. "This only brings me back to square one. Every time I think I can trust someone or confide in them some deep, hidden, secret rears its head. I'm exhausted. I just want to know what happened to Blake and why. Everything else can just go fuck itself."

"Look," Trent says, rubbing the back of his neck with his free hand. "I don't do all this feeling shit. I said my piece last time. If you aren't sure whose honest then don't trust anyone. You and McCall though... Blake flipped out initially. He trusted McCall. McCall didn't plan on having those feelings about you though either, and I think they both got to a place of respect about that before we even got to Vegas that day. They tabled their differences because in the long run, you were what was important to both of them."

"For not doing feelings you sure had some flowery phrases in there," I answer, making a gagging noise. In reality, Trent's little pep talk moved the earth beneath my feet again.

"You and McCall need to figure your shit out," he says, clamping the cigarette stick between his teeth. Trent's hand reaches out and pushes my hair away from my neck. My cheeks tinge pink, Jay's bites are very visible, while I keep my face impassive. He chuckles and lets my hair fall back into place.

The races start to die down below, the crowd's tell-tale cheering signaling that they're over. "Take the south path back. No one goes that way," Trent instructs before blending back into the shadows. Shivers cascade down my body. Twisting my fingers into the sleeves of my brown leather jacket, I slowly make my way to the southern path, avoiding boulders and people along the way. It's a quick jog to my car from there and I drive away easily, finally able to relax.

About a mile down the road, my grip eases off the steering wheel, driving back into town.

"Keep going straight." His voice is husky and smooth in my ear, instantly sending my heart pounding against my rib cage. It's been a day without a word from Jay and now we're sharing the small space of my car. His fingers flex at the side of my neck where he holds me in place, sending shock waves over my nerves. My pulse leaps under his touch, fire spreads rapidly throughout my body and pools in my core.

"Where?" I choke on the word, swallowing past the instant heat and need coursing in my veins.

He places a feather-light kiss right below my ear. "Stay on this road, north. I'll tell you when to turn." Unable to speak, I nod and try to calm my breathing back down.

"Turn the music on, Blaise," he instructs, my name rolls off his tongue and sends butterflies off in my stomach.

I slip in my favorite CD and adjust the volume. Jay's grip eases off my neck. His knees brush against the back of my seat as he slumps down again. "Feels like driving with Blake," Jay mutters, but I hear him.

"It's his playlist." My eyes search the rearview mirror for a glimpse of Jay. He's hidden in the shadows and I can barely make out the smirk on his lips.

"Late nineties and early two-thousands rock was his favorite. He always joked that music after that was a waste. He also preferred making his own CD rather than using Pandora, iHeartRadio or Spotify," I tell him. Jay doesn't respond, indicating to me he already knew.

My throat thickens with emotion. "As a rule of thumb, I don't listen to the radio, ever. It's garbage and full of ads. I prefer to use an app to find music that fits my mood. That's where all my playlists come from." Silence hangs between us, our breathing in sync. Three Doors Down's "When I'm Gone" plays in the background.

"I didn't know that," Jay responds, his voice low and thoughtful. My heart soars again.

We don't speak the rest of the drive. The miles fly past along with the time. The entire CD plays and I start it over one more time before Jay instructs me to take an exit. The clock reads quarter to two in the morning. We've been driving for an hour and a half and my adrenaline is wearing out. I'm exhausted and now I have no idea where I am.

"Take a right at the stop sign," Jay instructs from the back. His voice is scratchy and gruff, I wonder if he fell asleep. Jerk.

"Take this road down until you hit Mason Street then turn left." I follow his direction until we hit a gated development.

"Where are we?" With the street light illuminating my car, I finally catch his eyes in the mirror.

"I stay here when I'm not needed at the Vegas office," he replies.

"So you live here?" my questions unanswered.

"Here." He hands me a badge that I hold in front of the screen. A few seconds later, the gate unlocks and swings open. Cautiously, I maneuver us through the gate and follow the winding road.

"Take a left here, then mine is third on the right," Jay tells me. The row of homes are all the same, tan with a reddish hue, white trim, and green turf instead of grass on quarter-acre lots.

"Geez," I mumble. "I wouldn't want to stay here either."

Jay grunts, opening his door and climbing out before I even shift into park. I grit my teeth, holding back when I really just want to tell him to go to hell. Is this considered kidnapping? Or carjacking?

"What are we doing here?" I ask once we reach the door.

"Talking," he answers, pinning me with a dark glance that sets my nerves on edge. Jay enters the code into the keypad before it unlocks. "Don't touch anything," he warns before we walk in.

"Right," I respond sarcastically. We step into the main room and then everything makes sense. If the loft was a surveillance camp, then this house has to be the hub of operations. All windows are blacked out, sheets of clear plastic wrap hang from the ceilings.

Seven different monitors sit in a clump, each screen depicting a different screen.

"Oh my god!" I gasp, my face turning pale. On one of the screens is Marco's home, a party is still in full swing. The footage is of the back room where the guys usually gather. My eyes dart to the next, showing footage outside Stone and Antonio's duplex. A few cars are parked outside, none of them I recognize. The others are of various other locations, including the front of my own house.

Jay clears his throat. "It's pretty self-explanatory. We run the feed here and our IT experts go over the audio. Over here..." He directs me to the area where the kitchen should be. "Any evidence that has been collected, footage, and stills go on this timeline."

My eyes follow where he points along a red string from cupboard to cupboard. Dates, times, pictures, addresses and sometimes numbers are all marked with bright colored sticky notes. It's a giant floor to ceiling map and collage. I've never seen anything like it. "What do the ones in red mean?" I ask, paying close attention to the dates and times.

"This one here is the time and location of Blake's cell phone when he called me to change the plan, this one here is the incoming and outgoing calls between Seth and Blake, and this is the last call and location that Blake made to me. Each is time-stamped so we know how long the call was open. And these ones in green are the communication logs, and surveillance from La Flor hotel, your home, the loft, Garcia's condo, and the only road camera from the last stoplight before hitting town. Basically, this is the life of this case." His chest heaves with a sigh.

"Some of these dates go back over five years ago," I comment, my eyes dragging over everything, trying to commit to memory. "No way, is that Trent?" I ask, pointing at the younger version of the man, a cocky smile playing on his lips while he stands next to a pimped out motorbike.

"Yeah," Jay responds. "Before he lost his sponsorship."

"That was because of this case." I quirk my eyebrow at him. Jay nods his head yes. No wonder Trent had a chip on his shoulder.

My eyes dart to the billboard and the three photos in the center. The one on the left is of a middle-aged man, black hair, cropped at the sides and slicked to the side. His goatee is peppered with grey. The man is walking to a parked, blacked-out SUV and carrying a large briefcase. His suit screams money and designer brands. His face would be considered handsome, silver fox, if it weren't for the stone-cold evil of his eyes. "Who's that?" I ask even though I have my suspicions. He's almost familiar, like a distant echo of a memory.

"Raul Alverez," Jay confirms, which sends goosebumps down my arms. "His daughter." Jay motions toward the next picture. "Scarlet Reyes."

Reyes and Alverez, the two names I've been dwelling on since my return.

"He's her father, but why do they have different names?" I ask. The woman in the picture is stunning. Her long dark hair reaches to her waist, dark arched eyebrows are perfectly shaped over large brown eyes. Her lips are painted a deep red that complements her skin tone. She looks relaxed, the picture intimate in a way.

"Bad blood," Jay responds, shrugging. "She took her mother's maiden name, I guess."

"This picture wasn't taken with surveillance. She's looking at the camera. Who took it?" My curiosity getting the best of me.

"The poor sucker whose career she helped destroy," Jay replies. Obviously there are harsh feelings there, too.

"Wait!" I exclaim, pieces falling in place. "Reyes is the one who set up Trent?"

"Perceptive." Jay smiles, hip checking me before leading me to the staircase.

"No way," I go on. "That really explains so much. So that means they're cartel then, doesn't it? Then the last picture without the face, how do they fit in?"

"Wish I knew, babe," he says, opening the door into a room with a bed and dresser that connects to a bathroom. "That is the unanswered question."

"The person you're trying to find," I state. Jay sits on the bed, cradling his head in his hands, nodding. For the first time, I realize how tired Jay looks. His clothes are wrinkled and over a week's worth of facial hair is growing in. Purple smudges sit under his brown eyes. "Jay—"

"I know," he cuts me off. "I know we have some fucked up things to work through and talk about. I will talk. I'm just exhausted right now."

I walk toward him until I'm standing in the space between his legs. "How about a hot bath, then sleep?"

He cocks his eyebrow. "Only if you join me."

I swallow past the lump of relief in my throat. "Okay."

Jay takes my hand in his and leads me into the bathroom. He runs the water before stripping us both bare. The tub is big enough for us both, and I lay comfortably reclined against Jay's warm, bare chest. "Blaise?" My name rolls off his tongue in question.

"Hmm?" I reply, laying my head back, my eyes fluttering close.

"Tell me about Vegas." His voice is stern, but not demanding. He wants to know and finally I'm ready to tell him. I apologize about how I left and why I made the decision. I explain the car ride and the day and night I spent in Las Vegas with the guys. It's not sugarcoated and I hold nothing back, giving Jay all my truths. He tenses when

I reveal I was drugged, his fingertips turn white from gripping the edges of the tub while I tell him about the next morning and how scared I was. "I wanted you to be there and knew right away the mistake I made. I didn't mean to hurt you, Jay. I shouldn't have lied. I thought I was doing the best thing, and I don't know, helping in some way."

He cradles my chin between his fingers, turning my face to his. "You're one of the strongest people I know, Blaise. You've been through hell and none of this has been easy on you and every day you get up and keep fighting. I get you want to see something happen and you want to help. If the guys didn't have a history with you though… I'm scared about what could have happened."

"I know," I tell him, tears blurring my vision. "It was stupid. I'm sorry."

Jay's lips touch mine softly before pulling back. "I'm sorry, too. I didn't want you to find out the way you did and that's why I got angry the other night. I swear on my life I was going to tell you after the case. Before fuck-face beat me to it."

"I think Seth thought he was protecting me," I tell him. Jay scoffs. "We're all in the dark, Jay. Seth has limited information to work off of, too. No one knows who to trust or who's waiting to stab the other in the back."

"We can talk about Baird later," Jay answers, rolling his eyes and I stifle a laugh. "Let's get some sleep." He pulls me to stand and each of us takes one of the towels we laid out. We dry off and I borrow a pair of boxers and an Academy t-shirt from Jay before joining him under the covers. He's asleep before I even lay my head down. Smiling, I inch closer, until I'm burrowed right next to his side. My name slips between his lips in his sleep but he doesn't wake up, which makes my heart beat double time. Smiling to myself, I pull the blanket tight and fall asleep.

———————

My mind is fuzzy a few hours later. Cracking my eyes open, I momentarily forgot where I was and how I got there. My arm stretches out toward Jay only to meet empty space.

"Jay?" I shoot up, clutching the blanket to my chest. Slightly pissed he wasn't here when I woke up. I climb from the bed and make my way downstairs. My jaw drops and I swear a trickle of drool escapes while I take in the sight before me. Jay, shirtless, with only a pair of light grey sweatpants riding low on his hips. I watch fascinated while his back muscles flex and twitch while he scoots the mouse around by the monitor. My mind wanders back to the bed we slept in and what I wouldn't give to have his body over mine, raking my nails down his perfectly sculpted back while he feeds his body into mine.

The monitors crackle to life, shocking me from my sex-induced daydream. The blood in my veins turns icy when voices I recognize play through the speakers.

"This weekend?" Joe's voice bounces off the walls.

"Yup," Toni answers him. "He wants us there Friday night again."

"It's the third time this month already!" Joey argues.

"We do what we're told," Stone interrupts them. His voice cold and calculating. "If you have a problem, you know the way out."

Joey visibly swallows on the screen. My pulse races watching and listening to their exchange. "I don't like it." He shrugs.

"No one asked for your opinion, Joe," Stone replies.

The screen turns to static after that. "What happened?" I stride farther into the room until I reach Jay's side. He's watching, his jaw cupped in his hand. "I'm not sure."

"Sounds like they're going to Vegas again," I muse.

"I thought so too at first, but they've only been there once and that was with you." Jay stretches, walking over to the kitchen. "I made coffee." He points me toward the machine. I pour a cup while he examines his timeline and going over his notes. His hair is longer on top than usual. Another sign that he hasn't been taking care of himself.

"You need a haircut," I tell him while taking a sip of coffee.

He smiles. "Anything else?"

"You need to shave." I point to his chin.

His eyes darken as they trail over me. "I think you'll be thinking differently later when I'm wrapping your legs around my neck," he warns. His words turn my cheeks pink and it suddenly feels warmer in the room. I look away, unable to keep eye contact, which only has him laughing at my expense.

"How about food?" I ask, desperate to change the subject.

"I figured we'd stop at the café in town on our way back." He shrugs.

"We're leaving soon?" My chest deflates. Being out of that town and with Jay is the most relaxed I've felt in months. I can finally breathe and think clearly. Plus, I have a fine as fuck man to keep me occupied.

"I think we need to talk about a few things before we leave," he concedes. My stomach drops in response. I'm a bundle of nerves now.

"Okay." My voice is stronger than I feel while I fight to keep my hand from shaking and put my coffee cup down. I lift my head to meet Jay's gaze. Internally, I'm a hot mess ready to melt into a puddle at his feet. I school my features into a calm mask and remind myself to breathe.

"I thought about what you said about Baird. Trent has been able to keep better tabs on him and agrees with you that it may be best to bring him in. Find out what he knows. Then we figure out what we're missing," Jay explains, his eyes intently roaming my face.

"You also get the money," I remind him gently. Jay nods even while his lips thin in a frown. I can tell he isn't thrilled to have Seth join us, but it's the right thing to do at this time.

"If something goes wrong, I don't want you to be there," he tells me.

I snort. "Not gonna happen. I'm coming."

"Blaise." Jay's eyes close. "I'd die if anything happened to you. I don't think you fully understand the magnitude of how I feel about you. You're mine and I can't lose you."

"Jay." I swallow, looking down at my toes. "I need to be there. We can have a plan, I'll stay by you, anything, but I can't not be here."

Jay's body invades my space before I can inhale my next breath, his large hands cup my face, forcing my eyes to his, reading my secrets and exposing my soul to him. "Why do you need to be there?"

I lick my lips, biding my time. "I want to know what happened, and…" My voice trails off. I swallow repeatedly past the burn in my throat. "I don't want anything bad to happen to you."

"Why?" He forces and pushes me more.

"I care about you," I whisper.

Jay's mouth slants over mine, gliding and biting my mouth into submission. I open for him, his tongue dives in, tangling and stroking with mine. Jay pulls my body into his, one hand wound around my ponytail, anchoring my head in place. His other grips my hip, forcing our bodies together. My arms wind around his neck, forcing me to stand on tiptoe. Jay cradles me to him, feasting on my mouth. A rush of warmth settles between my legs. I pull my mouth away from Jay's, trailing a hot path of kisses across his jaw and down his neck. I pay him back in bites, pulling the sensitive skin between my teeth until he groans. I'm unable to hold back and drop to my knees, tugging the band of his sweatpants until his long, hard cock springs free.

"Blaise." His voice is filled with warning and need. It's all I need before taking him in my mouth. He groans, his head tilts back while his throat bobs up and down. He's under my spell. I'm in control, with his hand twisted around my already messy hair, his grip tightening with each suck and lick from my tongue on the underside of his dick. My eyes water when he pushes deeper. I keep my mouth suctioned, a thrill of excitement and need races through my body, sending another wave of heat between my shaking legs.

"Fuck," he murmurs, looking down at me, his eyes black with pleasure. He fists my hair tighter until the edges of my scalp burn, bringing my face closer to his pelvis. Sweat and tears mix down my cheeks when he hits the back of my throat, sending a hot jet of salty release down my throat.

Jay slips easily from my mouth, gently using my hair to pull and guide me until we're face to face. His lips coast over mine gently. "I'm never letting you go," he tells me. I pull back, my eyes wandering over his face. His cheeks are flushed, his pupils are dilated and a look of absolute determination settles over his features. Too stunned to speak, I nod my head instead. My heart swells with the love I feel for this overbearing, sexy as hell man, while at the same time my stomach drops. We're in deep, and I know I won't survive if I lose him.

Fifteen

I T's ALMOST DÉJÀ VU WHEN I FIND myself at the Look Out less than twelve hours later standing next to Trent. This time he wears a smug grin on his face when he sees Jay's arm wrapped protectively around my waist, with his large hand gripping me. I flip him off, which only earns me laughter from both of them.

"'Bout fuckin' time," Trent says, eyeing me as if he's waiting for me to tell him that I really want this. I nod in response and for some reason, my eyes fill with tears.

"Baird not here, yet?" Jay questions, looking around, before meeting Trent's gaze.

Trent shrugs. "His tracker is five minutes out."

"Tracker?" My brows raised in shock.

"It's a precaution," Jay answers for both of them. "Last thing we need is for him to slip away again."

"Still," I admonish. "Isn't that a little much?" They both frown at me. "He's here to help us. He's ready to give the money, now that he knows who he can trust."

"Yeah, after he took off and has been off the radar for months," Jay bites back, his eyes narrowing.

"So, you really don't trust him then?" I demand, slightly pissed we're still at a crossroads over this. "Why are we even here then?" I move out of his embrace despite the slight chill in the evening air.

Jay pinches the bridge of his nose between his fingers. "Come here."

"No," I retort, moving farther away.

"Blaise." Jay's voice deepens. My name on his lips a command. I lift my chin defiantly.

"No," I repeat. "I'm serious. You said we're all on the same side. Why would you be tracking him? Are you tracking all of us?"

They both go silent. Trent turns his attention to the action by the track. My stomach drops when Jay's mask slips into place.

"You," I start to ask before my mouth closes. I'm not even sure what I'm trying to ask. "You didn't, right?"

Jay turns away from me, his voice icy and full of authority when he speaks. "Yes, when you got back from Vegas."

"Like he said," Trent interjects, finally turning to position himself between us. "It's a precaution. Things are still dicey right now."

"How is any of this supposed to work if we aren't trusting each other!" My voice hisses at Jay.

"It's not about trusting you," Jay barks back. "It's about making sure you're fucking safe every hour of the day."

I ignore his statement and the way my chest tightens. "Then, why Seth, too?"

"It's okay, Blaise, I already know." Seth emerges from the shadows and walks toward our little group slowly. His arms are raised in surrender, a black duffle bag clutched tightly in one of his hands. Trent moves toward him, patting from his ankles to his chest.

"Turn," Jay commands. I'm seething by now, watching this play out, watching Seth being treated like a traitor. As if he can read my thoughts, he throws me a wink before turning for Jay and lifting his black t-shirt above the waistband of his jeans.

"Clear," Trent mutters, gently removing the duffle bag from Seth's grasp. He turns back to face us, his face tight and grim.

"Everything's in there," he addresses all of us but his gaze is trained on Jay. Several heartbeats pass while they silently size each other up. I'm about to lay into Jay again when he finally nods.

"What happened?" he asks, his voice crackling like sandpaper.

I notice Trent's body stills as if he's waiting on bated breath to hear the story. My own heart stops then speeds up again and I realize I want the whole story, too. These three can finally piece together everything I've been missing for the six months.

"Are we good to talk here?" Seth asks, nodding toward the track.

"Races are over, it's just the stragglers left, people passed out." Trent lifts his shoulders, confirming we're alone.

Seth takes a deep breath in and exhales, taking a few steps back until he can lean against the boulders. "I was waiting where I was supposed to be. The car was ready in case things went bad. About half an hour before the meet, Blake shot me a text saying that things weren't right. He and the guys were all split up for the job, which never happened, we always worked together or at least with one other person. They also had him on rooms instead of the club or the streets. He met me at the garage and tossed me the bag. He said it would be better if everything was split up. We decided to meet at the pit stop between here and Vegas. He was trying to call Trent first." Seth stops and slides his focus to Trent.

Trent nods. "He did. My call log was eleven thirty-five p.m. On his room detail, he was told Alverez would check on his progress and assign further information. We talked about this being a red flag. Alverez would never make a face to face with runners."

"Alverez is the guy from Mexico, right?" I ask Jay quietly, bringing the image of the photograph in Jay's house from my memory. I shiver again, remembering the man's soulless eyes. Jay nods at me.

"Then what?" Jay questions, turning back to Seth, his face set in a serious expression causing him to look like the detective he is supposed to be. My mouth drops open and I snap it closed again quickly, unsure how this makes me feel. It's one thing to hear it but entirely daunting to see the evidence in front of my face.

Seth rakes his hands through his hair, his face falling, and for the first time, I notice how truly exhausted he looks. "I drove right to the pit stop. He wasn't there when I got there. My route only took me an extra twelve minutes, which we knew would happen. He agreed to wait. I waited. Thinking maybe he got pulled over or something, or he got a hold of you, or I don't know. I didn't have your number so I called Nichols…" His voice trails off.

"My call log was one twenty-two a.m.," Trent states. My heart continues to hammer away, my anxiety eating away at my insides while they piece together the timeline on the last few hours of Blake's life. Tears form and gather at my lower lashes yet I refuse to let them fall. Blake's crash happened at three forty-eight a.m. Sergeant Ramirez knocked on our front door at five to deliver the news. Not once in this story has anyone said my brother didn't do what he was supposed to do.

"Actual time of death was three eleven a.m," Jay tells us, the anguish on his face replaced with anger. "His last call was to my phone at three-ten."

"You talked to him," I repeat back. Jay had told me before he talked to Blake before his death but not that he talked to him right as he was dying.

"All I could hear was scuffling, some muffled voices, then the line went dead," Jay answers. "I didn't call back in case they just took him, I didn't want to give them anything to torture him over. The crash was called in thirty-five minutes later."

"So, somewhere in a span of four hours, give or take, he left Vegas, stopped at the pit house, we think, and ended up back a little bit outside town where he crashed." My brain fights to compute every detail from what we heard.

"A lot can happen in four hours," Trent replies, his voice almost robotic, as if he has spun these details in his mind thousands of times.

"Were there trackers then?" I ask.

Jay's eyes narrow and Trent shakes his head no. "Trust," he responds and I slam my mouth shut, forced to eat my words from earlier.

"And how do all these other people play into this?" I turn to Jay for the answer, sensing he's trying to hold back, a nagging in my mind, and I can't let up. "And, if all the guys were in Vegas, how did they make it back in time without being seen?"

"Antonio wasn't in Vegas," Seth answers. My eyes swing to him, watching as he almost zones out. His complexion paling while the memories click into place. "I can't believe I forgot that. He left Saturday morning. His mom was sick. That's why it was first mentioned we would split up."

I turn back to Jay accusingly. "You knew this little nugget of information already?"

He nods at me, his mouth set in a grim line.

"Alverez is cartel from Mexico. He supplies Mamacita to different clubs in Vegas. His daughter, Scarlett Reyes, is his go-to person. She does all his appearances and deals," Seth tells me, answering my question from earlier. "All our deals with them started out easy. Just deliver the drugs and get the money. We were nameless, faceless, and it paid big."

"Then how did it change?" I step closer to Seth, forcing his eyes to mine. All our memories together flash through his eyes and right to my soul. The person I loved first is gone and replaced with this broken individual in front of me.

"I was sick that summer off and on so I didn't go with. They still went though because there was a rumor that the payouts would be almost triple. Alverez was talking about opening his own casino. When Blake got back he was different. Withdrawn, the guys were barely talking and when they did it was almost in code. I asked Stone what his problem was and he threw punches instead. I said fuck that, basically, and refused to go anymore if they were going to hide things. I started my part time job around the same time and they drug tested." Seth states.

"You know what happened?" I turn to Trent, who, in turn, looks to Jay.

"Let's talk about this part later," Jay responds. "We all know what happened. I'll tell her later." His voice is tight and I can tell he's close to losing it. We've been doing a lot of sharing. Even while I still see holes in everyone's stories, I force myself to stop talking. Seth looks close to passing out, Trent has completely shut down and withdrawn. He's not even present anymore and Jay has probably ground his teeth to pegs by now. I step back into my own space before my legs move on their own toward Jay. When I'm in arm's reach, his hand shoots out, snatching my jacket and pulling my body into his. Seth's eyes flicker with pain, but I can't stop the waves of peace that washed over me instantly. I try to ignore how that makes me feel only there is no denying it. I love Jay. I couldn't make myself tell him this morning. Tonight he was willing to share and let me lead the conversation. I'm grateful and another small piece of closure has slid into place.

"You're with me." Trent motions to Seth for him to follow. We watch them leave, not moving or talking. When we're alone and can no longer hear the crunching on the gravel, Jay turns me in his embrace.

"Your place?" he asks, looking to me for direction.

My tongue suddenly feels thick in my mouth. "Yeah." He nods and takes my hand, leading us down the same path Trent set me on before.

When we get to the clearing, Jay's bike sits waiting for us. "We took your car here though," I remind him, confused.

"I know, precaution," he replies, handing me an extra helmet. I don't even question or second guess him this time. Instead I slide the helmet over my head before swinging my leg over the bike and settling behind Jay's frame. I wrap my arms securely around his middle when the engine roars to life. He takes off, the momentum pushing my body into his. My eyes close and I breathe in and out. Before I can fully relax, we arrive at my building and I'm suddenly on edge again.

"You okay?" Jay asks before grabbing my hand in his and leading me toward the door. I shrug, even while dying inside. Too much has happened in the past seventy-two hours and I have no idea how much more I can take. I unlock the door and lead him inside. Jay takes one step toward the kitchen and I know he sees it. My mom's letter. Her resignation of being my mother.

He turns to me, crumpling the paper in his hand. "Please tell me this bullshit isn't true?"

"We said no lies," I answer, meeting his heated gaze.

A flush creeps along his cheeks, his eyes narrow. "Fucking bitch," he spews. "She actually left you? Here?"

I look away from the intensity of his gaze, wrapping my arms around my middle. His words hurt even though I know he's concerned. "All her things are gone," I confirm for him. My mind rejects the idea again. How a mother not only voluntarily leaves her only living child but *wants* to leave is beyond me. How sick and selfish is the person who would do that?

I wait for Jay to speak. I can feel his eyes on me, watching, roaming everywhere while he reads me. Minutes go by before either of us speaks. Suddenly he moves past me, stalking down the hall until he reaches my mom's room. The door whips open and I jump where I'm standing. From here, the echo of drawers being open and closed. My eyes have already seen the evidence yet I can't stop my feet from shuffling forward toward the scene again. Jay storms out, almost colliding with me in the process.

"Let me stay here," he commands, his hands cradling my face between them. My lips part in surprise. His forehead comes down to rest on mine. His scent surrounds me, easing the tension in my body. "I want to be here with you all the time," he tells me. I want the same thing.

"I want you here," I agree before pushing my lips to his softly. Jay continues to cradle my face and brushes his lips against mine gently, in tune to my need for comfort.

"I want to clean out Blake's room," I tell him, pulling away from his lips.

"Right now?" he asks, stepping back, the concern in his eyes multiplies.

I nod. "I know it's late, but I can't sleep. My mind is on overload right now. There isn't much in there anyway. We can just drop it off at the storage unit."

"Okay," he agrees even though he probably thinks it a bad idea.

I don't know what I expect to happen when I open the door to Blake's room, but it's not how I imagined it either. We make our way into the room with a box each. Jay starts removing the bedding while I take the posters and pictures down from the walls. When we moved out, Blake had already removed his clothes from the dressers and they sat empty. I open and close them regardless. Jay moves over to me, pulling out the bottom drawer until it slides off the track. He turns it upside down then feels underneath. Silently, we each work our sections of the room, overturning and looking under, until we reach the desk together.

"That's a cute picture." Jay nods to the framed image of Blake, Seth, Joey, and I. Our faces are tan, our smiles big and unworried. It was the first summer in years that we felt like we had a family. Blake has one arm around Seth, whose arm is slung around Joey. Joey is flashing a rock sign at the camera. I stand in front of all of them, my grin the biggest. He picks it up, popping the frame off and looking inside. I've done the same thing so frequently I know he won't find anything.

"We made a treehouse on Sarge's property that summer. We spent so much time out there Pricilla started calling it our Neverland," I tell him. The nostalgia hits me like a tidal wave forcing my torso to bow under the pressure. "We were so close. They were family," I mutter through the emotion squeezing my throat.

"People change, Blaise. Money also changes people. These guys had the chance to make the kind of money they've only ever dreamed about," Jay tells me, his finger swiping away the tears before they slide down my cheeks. "I thought maybe it would be here," he tells me.

"I know," I tell him. "It's only memories though." Jay watches me, taking a glance around us.

"Let's go to the storage lot," I suggest. Jay silently agrees and follows me out of the apartment.

My face is blotchy after spending the twenty-minute drive with silent tears streaming down my face. Jay carries the boxes from my trunk to the locked stall. I spin the combination on the dial and sigh audibly when it pops open. This time I don't even pretend to pack. I set the boxes from home onto the bench and slide to the floor while Jay goes through everything. We're silent while he works, which is both a curse and a blessing. I don't want to know what he finds suspicious, but then I'm also left alone with my own thoughts.

Time slips by while we're in there. I hear Jay's sigh that's laced with frustration before he slides down next to me. His arm shifts around my shoulders, cradling my frame with his. "Nothing," he murmurs into my hair.

I nod. "I know. I had hoped though maybe you would find something that I overlooked."

His brown eyes meet my blue watery ones. "I did, too," he tells me, confirming what I already suspected. "Just more memories."

"Too many," I agree, chuckling lightly. My eyes close and I feel Jay shift so that I'm half laying on top of him.

"Blake saw something really horrible, didn't he?" I voice the one thought nagging me all night. Jay's body stiffens underneath me. His chin rubs against my hair when he nods. I squeeze my eyes shut tighter, the pain in my chest amplifies until all my nerve endings are stinging in response. "I don't want to know," I tell Jay, tilting my face to his. "Blake worked hard to protect me from whatever it was. It was enough for him to seek you out and he tried his hardest to make it right. That's all that matters to me."

"Okay," Jay responds between placing light kisses on my left cheek, my forehead, my nose then my right cheek last. He tightens his grip on me before speaking again. "I lied earlier," he confesses and my stomach drops. I need to see his face, but he holds me immobile, trapped against him.

"I wasn't Blake's last call."

I glare, watching his throat bob. Jay shifts so that he can look down at me.

"He called you."

"He didn't," I challenge. "My phone never rang. I never had any missed calls."

"I know." Jay acknowledges my truth. "His phone never had a chance to connect, but he tried. Three seconds was on his call log. I didn't want to tell them. You deserve to know this. Blaise, you were his first and last thought always. From the moment he started working with me, it was all about you. He told me all about his little sister and how kind, funny, and brilliant she was. He wanted you to do better than him."

Fresh tears leak out of my eyes, a sob racking my body. "I miss him so much, Jay. I can't do this without him. I don't know what to do anymore."

Jay pulls us both to a sitting position, turning my body to face his so that our knees touch. His hands wipe away my tears. There is no sign of judgment in his eyes, only concern for me. "Blake was going to get a payout from this job. He denied the opportunity to use it on himself. He wanted a fund set up in your name. He told my director his younger sister was set on going to college. Blake wanted you to have that opportunity."

"He was so stubborn." I chuckle through my sobs. "That's so like him."

Jay smiles. "He just loved you and wanted the best for you."

"I know," I reply. "He was the only parent figure I had. He tried to balance it all."

"He was a good man," Jay agrees.

"Can we go home now?" I ask, peering at him through my lashes.

Jay's smile turns into a wolfish grin. "I love the sound of that."

I roll my eyes and climb up from the floor. I lock up the unit and we make our way back to the car. Jay's hands never leave my body, instead he finds any way to touch me that he can the whole ride back to the apartment. At the front door, Jay pulls a key from his pocket and lets us in. My mouth drops open, a protest on my lips until Jay captures my mouth with his. My hands come to his chest, pushing my face from his.

"The hell, Jay?"

"I'm not even sorry. I needed in. What if something happened or you needed me?"

"Still, not okay," I respond, anger quickly rolling in. "When?"

He can't meet my eyes at first. "When you moved back in," he finally answers, his gaze coming back to mine.

I'm speechless and taken aback. With all the new events, I almost forgot that Blake asked Jay to watch me. That Jay's always been watching me. Jay's known me longer than I've known him. My mind withdraws. Jay must sense the moment he's about to lose me again, his hands clutch my cheeks, bringing my lips to his before fusing us together. My hands are trapped between our bodies while his mouth does wicked things to mine. He bites and sucks at my lips until my legs are shaking, and my need for him to fill me throbs in response.

Jay guides me to my bed where my clothes melt away and his own joins mine on the floor. My back is cooled from the sheets while the front of my body is blanketed in Jay's warmth. He parts my legs easily and guides himself into my heat, not stopping until the tip of his dick hits my cervix, filling me completely.

"Jay." His name is a whisper and plea as it passes my lips. I want more. I need him in a way I've never needed anyone.

His arms bracket around my head, caging me in, while his lips tease mine. Jay starts to move over me, pulling back until he almost slides out before thrusting back in. Each stroke is deeper than the last, taking and claiming from the inside. My hands roam his back, clutching his body to mine, leaving small crescent indents from my nails in their wake. I wrap my legs around his waist, holding on while Jay makes love to me. My orgasm swirls deep inside, building more intense while Jay continues taking me, his lips never leaving mine. The release takes me by surprise, sending my back off the bed and curling my toes. I cry out loud against Jay's mouth. He groans in response before speeding up and chasing his own release.

"I love you." Jay punctuates each word with open mouth kisses over my neck and down across my chest before easing himself from between my legs. He rolls to his side, gathering my body into his. My mind has been effectively wiped and cleared. Everything from before pales in comparison to the feeling of having Jay hold me. My eyes flutter and close. *Jay has me wrapped tight and safe,* I think before falling into a dreamless sleep.

Sixteen

WITH ENCOURAGEMENT FROM JAY, I contact Jenna the next morning and ask for help covering a couple of my shifts. Between her and another new waitress, I'm covered for the rest of the week and Luis doesn't even argue with me when I call him to tell him the news. I've been an outstanding employee for the past three years. With the exception of the last few weeks, I've never taken time off. I swallow down the guilt I feel and try to remind myself what is at stake. After our discussion, Jay has moved in some of his clothes, shoes, and guns. His toothbrush sits next to mine in the bathroom and his towel hangs next to mine on the back of the door. Within hours of being awake, my fridge is stocked and I feel domesticated.

Jay makes me aware he needs to go to the operation site to check the cameras again. We shower together, saving the planet, all Jay's idea and I learn it's something I can definitely roll with. While he's gone, my job is to talk to the landlord about extending my lease and adding Jay. Our relationship has suddenly moved forward twenty paces and I'm nervous about struggling to keep up.

"It hasn't even been twelve hours," I remind myself while standing in front of the fridge deciding what to make for dinner. Jay texted fifteen minutes ago that he would be home in time and I suddenly want a Reagan-style meal just like on *Blue Bloods*. Once this whole case is over, I decide this will be a weekly event and I'll invite Trent, Seth, Jenna, and Logan too. My mind spins dream after dream for the future. For the first time in months, I feel as if I can finally move forward. I finally have a purpose and an idea of what I want. I also know college is in that dream, too. Hearing Jay confirm for me that Blake was planning to send me had made my resolve stronger to follow through. I can't wait to tell Jay what I've decided. I shoot him another text about dinner and having good news. A few minutes go by without a response. Shrugging, he did say he would be driving, I make my way around the kitchen finding everything for a low key meal.

By the time six o'clock rolls around, Jay isn't home and a pit of dread starts brewing in my stomach. I check my phone again to make sure I didn't miss any calls or texts. All my bars show I have enough service where something could go through. The chicken and potatoes I made for us are starting to cool. Pacing from the living room to the kitchen doesn't help the worry spreading in my veins. I gently pat my heart with my hand, trying to keep a level head. All he was supposed to do was go to the operation home and come back. I try to reason that if anything happened, Jay would try and contact me. And if he couldn't then Trent would.

By seven p.m, my nails are bit down to the nail bed and the entire meal I cooked for our first night living together is packed into the fridge. The sun has set, all I can see is darkness from the windows.

My call to Jay went to voicemail, which is also never a good sign. My text message to Trent and Jay both went unanswered as well. In a last-ditch effort, I call the only other person I can think of.

"Hello?" Sarge answers my call on the second ring.

"Hey, Sarge," I reply, starting to second guess myself. "Sorry to bother ya."

"Blaise? It's okay, are you alright?" His voice is thick with worry.

"Yeah, I'm fine," I reassure him. "It's uh… McCall I'm worried about. He isn't back yet, and not answering his calls or texts." A few beats of silence hang between us. I almost think the line went dead when he speaks again.

"Did something happen?" he asks, his voice quieter, almost whispering.

"He just went to his main base, but he said he'd be home two hours ago and I haven't heard anything. Like I said, he isn't answering texts or my calls," I explain, the panic growing thicker in my vocal cords.

"Did you try Nichols?" Sarge questions.

"Mhm," I respond. "Same deal."

I hear Sarge clear his throat gruffly on the other end. "I can try and reach out, but if something is going on, chances are that's why they aren't answering. Do you want me to put a patrol in front of your place?"

"God, no." I laugh. "I'm probably just being stupid. I guess I mostly wanted to know if something was going on I didn't know about."

"Nothing that I've heard, yet," Sarge states. "If anything does happen or you still don't hear from them in a few hours, let me know."

"Okay," I agree. "Bye Sarge."

"Adios," he answers before I click the end button. Holding my phone in my hand, I stare, willing it to vibrate. After a few beats, nothing happens.

"Fuck!" I vent my anger into the room, throwing my cell onto the couch. Something doesn't feel right, and it's taking everything inside me right now not to run from the apartment. I sprint to my room, throwing on a pair of jeans, hat, and black Converse. If I need to run, it will be more helpful. I make a deal with myself that if another hour rolls around and there is still no word, I'll pick up Seth and drive to the operation home.

In the silence, every noise seems to be amplified. My breathing comes in short pants, the creak across the floor echoes, and the buzzing from the refrigerator is like nails on a chalkboard. Chills trail down my spine causing my body to shiver in response. A vibration from my phone has me racing down the hallway to reach it. *Buzz, buzz, buzz.* Seth's name lights up the screen. My stomach bottoms out when I reach for it, swiping to answer.

"Seth," I almost yell into the phone.

"Blaise! They set me up!" His words are muffled, I can hear scuffling in the background. The phone sounds like it falls to the ground, his cries for help echo through the phone. It sounds like furniture is being moved and broken. A door slams before the line goes dead.

"Seth!" I scream into the phone, my hands shaking, and my body threatens to give out. I make it to the couch when I go down. Hands wrap around my shoulders and my body goes into attack mode ready to defend myself. Before a scream can tear from my throat, I'm turned in Jay's arms.

"Whoa." He grips me tightly. "Babe, what's wrong, what happened?"

Every emotion I've been fearing for the past few hours hits

me dead on like a freight train, and I lose it. "Where have you been? I think they took Seth! Oh my god, he sounded like he was kidnapped, why didn't you answer my call?" My chest rises and falls rapidly. I can feel the panic clawing its way out, strangling my neck, and threatening to tear me in half.

Jay grips me tighter, pulling me onto his lap while he sits in the chair. "Blaise, breathe. That's it, in and out." I try concentrating on the soothing circles his palm makes on my back, only Seth's frantic voice continues to fill my head. "What happened?"

He moves my head so we're eye to eye. "Seth," I breathe out. "He called me, and he was yelling. There was a bunch of noise. He said they set him up, but I don't know who or what he's talking about."

"He called you," Jay states, and I nod my head yes. Jay sighs, and his eyes slide from mine like he can't stand me looking at him. My heart freezes and I know the next words out of his mouth are going to change things between us. "I didn't have a choice. I was ordered to drop the hint. I didn't think he'd call you."

"You set him up?" Blood whooshes in my ears.

"I had to. I was given the order," Jay attempts to explain.

"Are you for real?" I stand up out of his reach, backing away. "Who knows what they're going to do to him? Why would you do that? Why wouldn't you tell me? Is that why you've been gone all day? Why didn't you answer my calls?"

His face goes blank, shielding me from the answers I'm seeking. In my heart I already know and the organ is shattering. There is a thin line between love and hate. He took the knife of betrayal and cut right through it. I just got Seth back in my life and who knows what happened to him. Jay specifically said the Alverez was cartel. All I can picture in my mind is Seth's head on a spike near the Mexican border. I feel sick, bile rising up my throat. After everything that happened yesterday, Jay went behind my back and made a call without consulting me or even warning me.

Before I can unleash the tsunami of anger welled up, the front door comes crashing open again. Trent's imposing frame fills the space. "We need to go."

My eyes slide over him. He's wearing dark jeans, running sneakers, and his usual racing jacket. In the light of my apartment, he looks less mysterious and more like a college roommate you meet for the first time.

"You were in on this, too?" I question, my voice now hoarse. My eyes flick between them both. They stand watching me, guarded, like they didn't just shred another tether of trust.

"We can explain on the way—" Trent starts to say, but Jay holds up his hand cutting him off.

"She's made her choice right now on which side she's on. Let's just get going." Jay brushes past me and down the hallway. A minute later, he returns, a small bag clutched in his hand while he's shoving his Colt into the back waistband of his jeans.

I stand immobile, tossing around my next steps. Jay's words cut me open as much as they infuriate me. He wants my trust, yet he acts before he explains or trusts me. Trent leaves first and I follow behind him. He jumps in the back of the idling blacked-out SUV in front of my apartment. Jay gets in the driver's side right as I slide in the front passenger seat. He doesn't speak and I turn toward the window to avoid him. Jay peels out of the parking lot and I'm vaguely aware of the static sound of a radio transmitter coming from the back seat. Jay drives us through town going over the thirty mile an hour limit. When he gets on the highway heading north, another round of anxious waves clash inside me. We're heading toward my nightmare, the place I just swore I never wanted to step foot in again.

"Vegas." The word leaves my mouth before I can stop it. Jay's grip on the steering wheel flexes, but he doesn't speak. Trent clears his throat in the back. The radio static breaks and a woman's hushed voice echoes in the small space.

"Alpha badge number 6-2-9, what is your current status?"

"6-2-9 riding. Arrival eleven hundred hours," Trent speaks into what looks like a walkie-talkie.

"Copy that 6-2-9, we'll show you arriving at eleven hundred hours," the woman's robotic voice responds back. The low hum of static continues on. My pulse races with adrenaline.

"Are we thinking this is going down at the hotel?" Trent asks Jay, who visibly becomes even tenser.

"That was the mistake we made last time." Jay's gaze flicks to the mirror. "Something still feels like it's missing."

"Let's split then," Trent responds, his voice monotone while his brain overanalyzes.

"Why do you need me?" I turn toward Jay. His jaw clenches and there's a slight flare to his nostrils.

"I need to know you're safe," he tells me without turning to look at my face.

"Well, I really don't trust a fucking thing you say," I fire back, daring him to challenge me.

"Can we put the brakes on this little lovers' quarrel until we get there?" Trent pipes up from the back seat. "All this tension is kind of turning me on. Makes it really hard to concentrate."

"Nichols," Jay fires back. "Shut the fuck up."

Trent laughs. "Don't be mad at me, big guy, because you chose to follow our assignment before you let her know."

"So, you were told to tip the guys off on where Seth was. To use him as bait?" I piece together the only logical explanation I can come up with what I've been given, which is absolutely nothing.

"I'll explain when we get there." Jay forces the words out between his teeth. I turn to look at Trent who already has his head laid back, earbuds wedged in, listening to music. Frowning, I turn back around and lay my own head back. I slam my eyes closed and try to concentrate on breathing. There is no way I'll actually sleep, but it gives me a chance to gather my thoughts. Twenty-four hours ago, we were all on the same side before something changed. Jay always has a motive, it's his delivery that sucks.

———

"Baby, we're here." I hear Jay's voice and my eyes flutter open. I hadn't meant to fall asleep and I wonder what else I missed while I was passed out. Yanking my arm from Jay's hand, I fling open my door and hop out. Trent is already grabbing the bag from the back and chuckles at the sour expression plastered on my face. Jay rounds the back and meets up with us.

"Where are we?" I ask, looking around the empty parking garage for any sign of a business logo.

"Hotel across from the La Flor," Trent answers, his voice low. He looks preoccupied while he says the words.

"You okay?" I ask him. His body looks wired, an almost frantic look hides in the depths of his gaze.

He opens his mouth to speak, until his eyes slide to Jay. Shaking his head, he walks away from us.

"What's that about?" I ask, not really expecting an answer.

"Some demons he has to face," Jay answers, shocking me.

"Is this about that Reyes chick? The one on the wall?" My brow lifts in question.

"She was the love of his life. He trusted her and she stabbed him in the back, then let him take the fall for her family's crimes. Trent went to jail, lost his sponsorship and was kicked out of the league," Jay explains, watching me intently.

"So, he wants payback," I state, trying to put myself in Trent's mindset.

"More like closure," Jay responds, tugging my arm so I follow him. The elevator sends us up, the doors opening to the lobby. People move about with their luggage, smiling and talking excitedly. They are oblivious to the situation I'm in, the danger that lurks not in the shadows, but in the very clubs and rooms they'll be staying in tonight.

Trent already holds two room keys and is heading back toward us. I reach out to grab one at the same time Jay does. "What are you doing?" I question. He's off his rocker if he thinks I'm staying with him.

"His key." Jay points to the purple card still in Trent's hand. "Our key." He waves the other in front of my face.

My arms fold over my chest. "I'm not staying with you. I want my own room or I walk."

"I'll throw you over my fucking shoulder if you even try," Jay grits out, stepping into my space and bringing his face to mine. My palm itches to slap him across his arrogant face.

"Okay, kids." Trent slides a hand between us. "Let's take this upstairs before we gain attention we don't need."

I follow Trent into a different set of elevators, conscious the entire time of Jay right behind me. Anger rolls off him in waves of heat, searing my back and setting flames to my insides. The minute we're off the elevator, the hallway splits in two. Trent heads down one direction. Jay grabs the sleeve of my shirt, tugging me in the other.

"Stop, Jay," I demand, struggling to pull away. "I'm not staying with you. I can't believe you did this after everything."

Jay stops and whips me around to face him. I'm momentarily blinded when my hair whips my face as well. "I will tell you everything, but first, we need to get into the room. I need you to trust me right now. You're pissed. I get it, but do you think I would do any of this if it wasn't important?"

"I honestly don't know anymore! Every time I think we've reached an agreement, shit like this blows up in my face. How am I supposed to trust you?" I throw back at him. Heat flushes my cheeks.

"You can't be serious right now. Everything I've told you and you're ready to cut and run now because Baird was picked up?" Jay's eyes darken. His gaze slants in my direction. The muscles in his chest ripple and his arms tense.

"I can't believe you lied to me that he would be safe. Who knows what's happened to him." My shoulders lift. I feel helpless and what's worse is I feel like I'm the only one who does care about Seth.

"Get in the room, Blaise," Jay demands. My body reacts and steps closer even though my mind screams that I shouldn't. Something isn't right, my gut warns me. My gaze flicks to Jay then my surroundings. The hallway is empty and too quiet. My eyes dart from the direction we came to the other end where an exit sign glows like a beacon of hope. Hairs on the back of my neck raise up and I feel my brother's presence. I dart past Jay, throwing my body against the opposite wall to avoid his grasp, my feet keep moving. A door crashes open behind me, but I keep running. Yelling and groans of pain bounce off the walls, a few sharp cracks and skin on skin slapping reaches me, yet I keep my eyes forward. My eyes sting from the air rushing past me and I blink from the pain. My chest expands with air and I blow out, pumping my arms. The ground shakes behind me, footfalls pounding against the carpeted floor. I reach the exit, bracing as my shoulder hits it hard enough to open. One foot over the threshold before a sharp pain radiates across the back of my head. My body is momentarily stunned, my adrenaline goes into protection mode fighting to keep the pain at bay. White sparks go off in my vision and I push my mind to stay conscious. My knees buckle and smack against the cemented stairway. Blackness clouds my vision around the edges, the ringing in my ears intensifying. I want to see who hit me, who is doing this, only I'm shoved forward. My hands don't react quick enough to break my fall. I turn my cheek just in time for my face to meet the ground. A popping sound echoes behind me. My head hurts, but the darkness is winning. My eyes close, not wanting to witness what comes next. I want peace. I want silence. I don't want to be here.

Seventeen

"**Y**ou can't catch us, Blaise," Blake yells back at me while he laughs. My little legs race faster, determined to make it to the top this time. I pump my arms in time with my feet, smiling when my body pushes forward.

"You might as well go home now," he continues to taunt and I realize we're running out of time. We're almost to the treehouse. Blake, Seth, and Joey built it this summer and teased me mercilessly that only boys were allowed. It was the first time ever that Blake wouldn't let me go with him and it broke my heart. I could do anything they could and it wasn't fair that they would kick me out. Treehouses are the coolest and I've waited all summer to go inside. Blake said if I beat him in a race he'd let me.

My pace increases or his slows down, and my heart swells thinking he wants me to beat him. I glance sideways, his grin turns to a smirk. The wind blowing through his thick dark brown locks. We break through the clearing at the same time. My arm reaches out to touch the tree first.

I'm determined to go with them. I want to be in Neverland. That's what Pricilla called it. They're the lost boys, and this place was their home, a place to escape. I remember feeling hurt when she told me that.

"Where's my home then?"

She smiled and ran her fingers over my braid. "With them," she answered.

My fingers brush the tree at the same time Blake's does. My hopes shatter. I turn to face him, ready to beg and plead to go up. His face throws me though. "Thought you'd never get here," he tells me. My eyes take him in. He's watching me, his brow furrowed in concentration. For some reason, I'm scared to speak. I just want him to keep talking. The sound of his voice comforts me. A nagging feeling in the back of my mind makes me nervous.

"You have to go back, you know," Blake says, reaching out to hold my hand.

"I don't want to," I tell him. It's scary without him. I'm lost and confused. "You won't be there when I wake up."

"I'm always with you, Blaise." He grips my hand reassuringly.

The trees and the ground start to disappear around us, a dull throbbing pain intensifying behind my pupils. "Blake," I whisper his name. Our matching blue orbs meet. He nods at me reassuringly. The ringing in my ears intensifies, white-hot pain flashing in my mind. My hands try to cover my ears.

"You're fucking crazy!" Joey yells. The sound of a solid punch follows and droplets of blood splatter my neck.

The back of my head throbs with a dull pain. My arms are bent at an odd angle, my wrists pinched by whatever holds them together.

"She's waking up, man." Antonio's voice pulls me the rest of the way back to earth. My eyes flutter open, my vision is tilted.

Rough hands grab my arms and haul me up to my feet. I sway instantly and am caught by Stone's solid chest.

"Time to be a big girl and stand up, Blaise." Stone's voice is next to my ear. I cringe away from the sound, forcing myself to look around the room. We're not in the hotel from what I can gather. The ground is cement smf the walls unfinished. Three construction lamps light the room up, casting eerie shadows.

"Help her fucking see what she's dealing with." Toni laughs. He sounds manic.

"Do you run the show, or do I?" Stone growls back. My gaze swings from Toni to Stone. Their pupils are dilated, beads of sweat gather on their foreheads and temples. Toni paces in front of us, the smile tugging his lips is sinister.

"'Bout time, little B." He claps in front of my face. I pull back, not recognizing the stranger in front of me. I've never seen Toni this way. I've seen him high on marijuana or rolling on some molly, but never this. His face hardens into a mask of pure evil.

"You smell good." Stone inhales against my neck and a new wave of goosebumps erupt over my arms. Cold metal touches my hand before Stone reaches down, wrapping my hand around the barrel of a metal Colt I recognize too well. "It's time to make a decision, Blaisey," he chuckles, his lips dipping down to touch the top of my bare shoulder. I try to shrink back, his hand winds around my back and pushes me forward.

My worst nightmare becomes a reality in that moment. Jay sits tied to a chair, gagged and immobile. A deep gash runs above his eyebrow, his nose is swollen, and blood coats the front of his shirt. His chair backed right up to another where Seth sits, tied and gagged. Bruises line his jaw, and crusted blood is dried under his nose. Seth watches me, his eyes wide. Jay rocks his chair, grunting and pulling at the binds.

"Control him!" Stone orders Toni who moves behind Jay, jabbing him in the shoulder with a pocket knife. Jay's face turns red then purple, his scream gagged by the fabric.

"Stop!" I yell, twisting away from Stone. He catches me quickly, hauling me backward. Lifting up our joined hands, he raises the gun toward Jay and Seth.

"Eenie, meenie, miny, moe," he sing-songs, swinging my hand back and forth.

"That's too fuckin easy," Toni taunts from the sidelines. "At least let her make the decision on her own."

"What are you talking about?" I turn to him. His smile spreads wider than the Cheshire Cat.

"Well princess… one of your knights in shining armor has been lying to you. The question is, who is telling the truth and who is not." Toni moves to Seth, sliding the gag from his mouth before doing the same to Jay. Jay spits bloodied saliva from his mouth onto the floor.

Seth's gaze finds mine, holding me hostage. "Blaise," he croaks.

"Ah, ah, ah." Toni shakes his finger in his face. "Little B needs to hear all the damage you've both done."

"What's he talking about?" My question is directed at Jay, who won't even look at me. His eyes trained intently on Toni, following him around the room.

"I killed your brother," Toni announces, stopping to stand in front of me. He sinks back so we're face to face. Tears spring to my eyes and trail down my cheeks, leaving a warm path along the way. "I wasn't alone though. He put up quite the struggle. It took two of us to pin him down before I could shove the needle into his arm. Hit the vein just right. This same person helped load him in the car and drove it toward the tree. Who could do such a thing?" His eyes glint.

"No fucking way!" Joey's voice bounces between us. For the first time, I see him seated in his own chair, tied, and a little bloodied. "You killed him? He was our brother. Family."

"No." Toni's voice goes high pitch. "We, are family." Toni motions between Stone and himself.

"You'd be in a lot better position, Joe, if you'd learn to keep your mouth shut and obey orders," Stone warns him. "There is no guarantee you'll make it out of here alive tonight either."

My heart races, bile rising in my throat, stuck behind the sob that's caught there. My mind spins with all this new information while my fight or flight instincts are triggering from the adrenaline.

"Alverez told you to do this?" Joey shakes his head in disbelief. In this moment, he reminds me of the character Stu from the original *Scream* movie. His version of reality shattered when he realizes his boss doesn't care about him and wants him dead. The fact that Joey couldn't see this as a possibility while working for the cartel makes me want to pity him. How naive to think you're untouchable when you're so low on the food chain in their world. Joey's face crumples like a five-year-old who just learned reindeer don't fly.

"Who was it, Blaise?" Stone asks, taunting me. "You can make it right, right now. Justice for your brother, right? That's why you've been hanging around the cop, working with him while pretending to give a shit about us."

"I did give a shit about you." I turn toward him. "Until I learned the truth."

"Didn't know you were sleeping with the enemy, did you?" Toni heckles. "Or is Seth the enemy? But wait, he's your first love, and he fucked you, too, so he couldn't do that to you."

Stone swings the gun toward Jay. "Seth and Blake were best friends. But did you know Seth here has a superiority complex? He'll never be as good as your brother. Maybe he did it?" Our joined hands move from Jay to Seth. The tears fall harder down my face.

"It's okay," Stone coos against my skin, shifting his body closer to mine. I can feel the hard length of his arousal as he grinds into my ass cheeks. I want to vomit, knowing this shit is turning him on. His fingers dance across my collarbone and dip into the space between my bra cups.

"Quit fucking touching her!" Joey yells at him, startling me in the process. I don't blink before Toni whips out his own revolver from his back, firing once at Joey. The impact sends his chair crashing backward. A pool of blood forming on the ground under him. I scream before Stone's hand clamps over my mouth. Gagging, I have to force myself to breathe through my nose, and shut my eyes trying to erase the past minute from my memory.

"I think it's Agent McCall," Stone announces over my whimpers and crying. "He's been leading you on with half-truths, hasn't he? Trying to turn you against your first love. Wanting you to believe he had no part in Blake coming back home where he died."

My head shakes in denial, rejecting the lies and the game. Stone brings the gun back to Jay. Jay's eyes are murderous, glaring, not an ounce of feeling in their depths while he watches us.

"Please tell me I'm not wasting money on this," another voice joins the conversation. A man steps from the shadows, dressed in an expensive-looking black suit and red tie. His black hair is peppered grey and styled to perfection. I instantly recognize him from the picture at Jay's home. Raoul Alverez. The air leaves my lungs. Heels can be heard clicking against the concrete next. Sky-high white stilettos step through the hanging plastic. The woman whose body follows next is his daughter, Scarlet Reyes. As stunning as her picture, she is almost identical to the slain Tejano music singer Selena. The pure white pantsuit hugs her legs and waist. The matching jacket hangs perfectly from her shoulders. The lace bodysuit underneath gives her the perfect balance of sexiness and business. My heart hurts for Trent.

"Can we just collect who we need and get out of here," she asks in accented English.

Shots fire behind me, Alverez's body crumples to the ground. Jay launches himself backward at Seth causing them both to hit the ground. Everything turns to chaos. Stone throws me to the ground, firing in the direction the shots came from. Alverez's men get in a few shots. Standing on shaky legs, I cradle Jay's Colt to my chest.

"Baby." Jay's voice calls to me in the fog. He stands in front of me, reaching out his hand, motioning for the gun. "Slowly, hand it to me. Do not squeeze the trigger."

"Blaise." My name from Seth's mouth sounds scratchy. "Don't. Give it to me. They set me up, we can't trust them."

My grip tightens, both hands cradling the handle. I rest my finger lightly next to the trigger.

"Look at me, Blaise," Jay commands and my eyes slide to him, keeping Seth in my peripheral. Shots continue to bounce around us. Focusing on Jay, I let the noise fade. "Trust me. You already knew I was here the night Blake died. He asked me to be."

"I know," I whisper, feeling a tug in my soul to believe him.

"Bullshit," Seth responds, pulling my attention back to him. "Blake knew things with your plan weren't right the moment we got there that day. He didn't trust you anymore and your sick obsession with his sister."

"He knew it wasn't right because his best friend that he brought on was taking calls from Alverez," Jay retorts. They've taken their concentration off me, now sizing each other up. Jay's face pales slightly. My stomach rolls watching Seth's face morph in front of me. His eyes slant, all humanity fading away, taking the memories of our childhood with it.

"Seth," I whisper, shaking my head in disbelief. His lips pull into a sneer. His body standing fully upright. He was never beat, and I was too stupid not to see it. "He was your best friend."

Seth barks out a laugh. "Friend? He left me high and dry in this piranha-infested tank. He knew I needed the money, my options were never as good as his. I wasn't going to college, this was the only option. He just had to keep his mouth shut about what he saw and everything would have been fucking different!" His hands tug at the roots of his long brown hair.

He lunges for me at the same time Jay dives toward him. My finger hits the trigger, my grip on the handle secure, my shot fires and goes over his head. Horror washes over me. Seth laughs. Another shot rings out, Stone crumples to the ground. Trent is propped on the floor, half in Reyes' lap, her hand holding the compact pistol that has been aimed at Stone. A third shot fires, my own hands jerk in response. My eyes meet Seth's. Disbelief slides in. The laughter on his lips turns to a cough. Blood oozes from the opening, painting his teeth and staining his lips. One hand clutches the chest area where my bullet is now lodged, the other reaches for me again. I step back and he falls to my feet.

"I'm sorry," I cry, sobs tearing out of my chest. Our gazes clash and for another minute, I see the lonely boy we met on the ranch when we were kids. Blake's best friend, my first love. The only other person I thought I could count on.

Jay rushes me, prying my grip off the Colt. He flips the safety on before shoving it in his waistband. He cradles me with his uninjured arm, shielding me the best he can with his body. I don't see Seth's last breath, or when his chest stops moving. My fingers dig into Jay's side, holding him tightly against me.

"I need to get out of here." Reyes' voice pulls our attention toward her. "Cops and ambulances are already on their way. I can't be here."

"You're not fucking going anywhere," Trent growls, his hand snakes to hers. He slaps a silver handcuff around her small wrist, then locking the other around his own.

"Are you out of your mind?" she screams, continuing to rant in Spanish. Trent looks like he doesn't know if he wants to shoot her or fuck her.

"You'll pay for your part in this," he hisses into her face. Regret and pain flash in her eyes, and I'm certain I'm the only one who notices.

"You don't know what you're doing?" she pleads, but Trent is stone deaf to her now.

Sure enough, sirens pierce the air. Jay leads me past the hanging construction plastic out a double set of iron doors that open to a garage. That's when I notice we're in the future parking ramp for La Flor. At least twenty squad cars and three ambulances greet us.

I'm pulled to an ambulance and I refuse to let go of Jay's hand, insisting he needs the medical attention more than I do. In the chaos and questioning, I lose track of Trent and Scarlet.

"They'll be fine," Jay grunts from his prone position on the stretcher, and I realize I spoke my concern out loud.

"I don't know, he looked like he could kill her." I lift my eyebrow challenging him.

"I don't think he actually wants to kill her. He loves her." Jay shrugs.

"She set him up," I remind him.

"She has her reasons. Reasons she needs to explain to him. They'll be fine," Jay assures me. I bite my lip, remembering the glare of hatred in his eyes when she wanted to leave.

"Wait..." Pieces start to click into place. "Her name is Scarlet?"

"Mm-hmm," Jay responds, hissing when the needle from the IV bag punctures his skin.

"Scarlet as in Scar. Is the track named after her?" The idea seems impossible and observed. I conjure Trent in my mind. SCAR is also tattooed across the knuckles of his left hand.

"They'll be fine," Jay repeats. "Just let it go."

"Or, he will kill her," I tell him dead serious. "That situation has Snapped written all over it."

"You're ridiculous, you know that." Jay chuckles and I flip him off. A yawn escaped me, and I cover my mouth in embarrassment.

"A lot of shit happened," Jay states, his finger tracing down my cheek, pushing the stray strands from my face. I nod. I want nothing more than to forget it happened. Blood is on my hands. I took a life and I panic wondering if Jay will still feel the same way about me.

"I'm proud of you," he answers.

"Did I say that out loud again?" I question. He nods, a breathtaking smile tugs at his lips. "I'm just going to shut up now. Don't ask me any more questions."

Our ride to the hospital is quick and they wheel us both into separate areas. I'm checked for any signs of a concussion and trauma. They ask if I want to speak to a therapist and I decline. No part of my body is broken, just bruised and strained. I'm told to drink liquids and I'm given a prescription for a stronger dose of Tylenol before I'm discharged. The minute I'm free, I set off to find Jay. I find out he's been admitted and his arm has a fracture. My hand lifts to knock when I hear his voice from inside talking with someone else.

"I can't give you clearance to stay here," the man's voice states. "You're already in violation for continuing a relationship with her."

My heart sinks.

"I'm not leaving," Jay responds. "We both know I didn't plan on falling in love with her, it just happened. I told you I was hesitant to come back and work the end of this case so close to her. It was your idea."

"Yes, for you to be close. Maybe take her to get coffee or dinner and get intel on those guys. Not live with her," the other man snaps back.

"I got intel just fine. You can't honestly be that surprised? I told you before the last case was over how I was feeling. Then you send me back here again. What did you expect?" Jay goes on.

"I'm assigning you back to Las Vegas upon discharge. Take a few days at least to think it over. Emotions were high on this case across the board. Palmer was a great asset to our team. He would have been a helluva cop. I can't help but worry that you're building this relationship off those emotions. She's young," the man finishes.

My heart jumps into my throat waiting for Jay to reply. I want him to deny what this man is saying. I'm confused and worried.

"Yes, sir," Jay answers back, his voice monotone.

"See you tomorrow then," the man tells him. His footsteps approach the door and I realize I'm about to be caught eavesdropping. Quickly, I duck behind a nearby curtain until the footsteps disappear down the hall. Peeking around the corner of the curtain, finding the hallway empty, I push open Jay's door. His gaze automatically jumps to mine. Love, concern, guilt, and some other emotion I'd rather not think about flashes between us. Is he confusing his feelings for me with this case?

"You look like hell," I tell him, trying to ease the tension. A small smile cracks his lips. His right arm is in a sling and his left shoulder is bandaged from where he was stabbed. The blood from his face has been wiped off. His nose and eyes though will be black and blue tomorrow.

"You look beautiful," he states to me and my cheeks turn pink. "Did you get discharged?"

I nod. "I wanted to check on you first. I can stay if you want me to." I bite my lip, hoping he'll agree to it. Hoping he'll tell me he never wants to be away from me.

"You should get some rest," he replies, concern dripping from his mouth. "I'll be fine tonight. Should be discharged soon, too."

"I'll wait then," I tell him, moving toward his bed.

"I have to go back to the Vegas office," he responds. "Paperwork needs to be filed and my report written. It might be a day or two until I get back."

"Are you coming back?" I ask, hating that I'm doubting him right now. A heartbeat passes before he answers.

"I want to," he responds. Not yes or no. He wants to. I nod again. I move toward the bed until I'm at his side. My lips touch his cheek and mouth before pulling back. Tears shine in my eyes and I let him see.

"I love you." The words pour from the bottom of my soul. His lips pull into a smile and his hand squeezes mine, but he doesn't say it back.

"You should get some sleep," he says again. My heart cracks at his words.

Without another word, I leave Jay's room. I'm tired, heartbroken, and everything feels worse than before. I'm glad Blake's murder has been solved and that those people are no longer here to hurt others. But a new hole in my chest has been ripped open.

Eighteen

THE LAST TIME IS FINALLY HERE. I poured the last beer on my shift at Señor Locos. After three years, I'm hanging my apron strings and moving forward. They say time heals and I say that's bullshit. My heart still bleeds every day for my brother. It's what I decide to do in my time to honor him that is bringing me closure.

I haven't heard from Jay in two weeks. The number I had has been disconnected. The loft he rented is empty and Roland confirmed he also no longer works there. Scar has been closed up for two weeks as well, causing a small uproar for the party community it served. The only communication I've had was the mysterious deposit that landed in my bank account. The total worth enough to pay for four years of my college education and the next month's rent until I officially move out. All his loose ends have been wrapped up in a pretty bow. My heart refuses to believe what my mind forces me to see. He's done, his case is closed, and what we had was a way for him to get close enough to solve Blake's murder.

I still cringe when I hear that word. He was murdered. The news was the biggest scandal in this small town in decades. People were shocked that not only was he killed, but at the hands of his closest friends. Guys that people had flocked to, couldn't start parties without and had generally seemed to be everyone's friends. Now they knew differently. Stone survived his gunshot wound and will be facing prison time. He's currently being held in a max security facility awaiting trial. Toni and Seth are both gone. I don't care what anyone says, to me it's justice. They didn't deserve to breathe the same air we do. Joey's wound nicked some internal organs and is lodged in his spine. He's in rehab, unable to move from the waist down. He's also facing jail time. Not that I care. They're all dead to me.

"How about a shot?" Jenna asks excitedly, bringing the tray of liquor over to me. Luis shut down early and opened only the bar to celebrate my last shift.

"Why not?" I shrug, taking the small glass from her. She raises her glass and the small, intimate group of people around us raise theirs, as well.

"To Blaise, everyone! To her success and nothing less!" Jenna shouts. "Cheers!"

"Cheers!" erupts around me. I down the golden liquor and suck the lime. Warm fuzzies spread from my fingers to my toes, but I know it's not just the alcohol. It's the wonderful group of people here, who stood by me in the darkest times of my life. I catch Sarge and Pricilla's eyes and smile. Jenna and Logan beam at me happily and Luis continues to clap. The celebration continues on for a few more hours. People I've known all my life stop by to congratulate me instead of expressing their condolences. I'm the last to leave besides Luis.

"If you don't leave now, I'm taking back your notice," he threatens. I scoff at him.

"You would, too," I joke, grabbing my wristlet from the empty chair next to me. "You sure you don't need help cleaning up?"

"Just get out of here." He shoos me toward the door. I stick my tongue out cheekily before sliding off my stool and exiting the building, smiling.

I don't even make it halfway through the parking lot to my car when I stop dead in my tracks. Jay's truck is parked next to my car, he leans against it casually. My insides tighten in response. His hair is cropped short again, the five o'clock shadow I love grown back in. His black jeans hug his thighs perfectly while the black t-shirt molds to his chest. His leather jacket hangs off him, making my mouth go dry. He's every woman's wet fantasy come to life, and he's waiting for me. I should run to him, let him swing me into his arms, and take me home. My legs won't cooperate though, the organ in my chest beats heavily from the pain we've experienced the past few weeks without him. My thoughts flip tricks in my mind spinning a lie where he isn't here to be with me but to officially end the torment I've been going through. That would be a Jay thing to do.

When he realizes I'm not budging, he pushes off the truck and stalks toward me. Every step he takes sets me on edge. Gasoline, leather, sandalwood and citrus assault my nose when I breathe him in. His gaze darkens when our eyes meet as if he can see my torment reflected back at him. When he's a breath away from me, I finally smell the mint rolling from his tongue when he speaks. "Can we talk?"

"I didn't think you would be coming back." I shrug, trying my hardest not to tear up and remain strong.

"It took longer than expected," he tells me.

"I tried to call," I say, making him aware.

"I had to get a new phone now that the assignment is over. I didn't want to have this conversation over the phone. You deserve more than that," he explains and I swallow past the hurt in my throat at his choice of words. *He's here to end us* floats through my mind, my subconscious laughs at the naive hopefulness I had been holding onto.

"Thank you," I tell him. "For what you did for Blake. It means more than anything to me that he can rest peacefully and to know the truth." I attempt a small smile, but my gaze turns watery. "I meant to tell you before, but things were crazy after the hospital."

Jay's eyes track over my face before he slants a dark look down at me. "Did you mean what you said at the hospital?"

My mouth goes dry, my veins simmering from his heated look. I know what he's talking about. It's on my tongue to lie and pretend I don't remember. Instead of shielding my already fractured heart, I nod. "Yes."

"Thank fuck," he responds before his lips claim mine.

His hands slide from around my face, down my arms, and around my waist, pulling me in tighter. After the initial shock wears off, my lips move greedily with his. Jay pours need and his love into this kiss, chasing my tongue with his, swallowing every moan that makes its way from inside me. I'm on fire everywhere when his hands grab my butt, and my legs automatically wrap around his waist. He turns and carries me over to the truck, sitting me in the bed, our lips never losing contact. My hands grip his shoulders, bringing his body farther into mine when he tears his mouth away from mine. Our eyes meet, his are sparkling with lust, his lips swollen from my kisses.

"You're not leaving me?" I bring myself to ask the big question. His lips form a grim line, his cheeks redden in anger.

"I'm never leaving you," he growls, the sound coming deep within his chest. "I'll follow you everywhere you go, protect you at every turn. I love you. Nothing will change that."

"I thought you weren't coming back," I tell him honestly, wanting to keep us on the right path of trust this time.

"I'm sorry. Everything really did take longer than I thought, considering we're still missing the main key points of evidence. I couldn't call you even if I wanted to." His hands move to cradle my face. "Nothing could keep me from coming back to you."

"I love you," I tell him, meeting the intensity of his gaze. It's apparent that's all he was waiting for. His lips dip down to mine, soft and strong, taking his time. When he pulls away, he brings my body into his. My arms circle his neck, holding him close in the hug and comfort I've been needing. Just past Jay's shoulder, my eyes catch quickly to the window of Señor Locos.

A shimmering form of Blake appears. He offers me a smile that speaks more than words. Love, sadness, understanding and finally a blessing. The Open light clicks off and he disappears. My eyes squeeze shut against the tears threatening to spring free. He's gone.

Sensing the change in my body language, Jay carries me to the passenger seat and sets me inside. I buckle myself while he hops in and drives us back to the apartment. Inside, my boxes sit in the living room taking up space. I don't officially move to campus for another two months, but I can't stay here anymore. Too many memories and I want to start fresh. I have a new apartment waiting off campus that I was able to move into. I'll be fresh and ready by the time spring semester starts.

Jay says little about the move as we lean against the kitchen counter. "UNLV, for sure?" he asks, his brow lifting in question.

After everything that happened, I was surprised, too. I swore I'd never return to that city. Shortly after though, I had a dream where I was wearing their white college sweatshirt and Blake's arm was around my shoulder while he joked at Jay's expense. It was a sign I needed and I signed my acceptance papers sending them along with the tuition money the next day.

"Yup," I tell him, feeling confident in my decision. "Now you'll have to see me all the time since we'll be in the same city."

"I can't wait," he answers, tucking a strand of my hair behind my ear. "I wanted to show you something. Now that Blake's murder is closed, I pulled this from evidence."

Jay hesitantly pulls a plastic bag from inside his jacket pocket. I recognize the phone immediately with its pizza slice phone cover. Jay pulls it out, powering it on. I stop breathing when it flares to life. A picture from our last Christmas together is still his screen saver. Jay opens the call log before handing the phone to me.

B outgoing 5/28/19 0:02

McJ outgoing 5/28/19 0:17

"He called you, too," I say. My eyes studying the screen.

"When we were at Scar, I started to piece together the time frame Seth was trying to feed us. He did leave Vegas when Blake did. Blake never went to the meet house. He came here, stashed the evidence and called me. I lied when I said all I heard was a scuffle because it was built of Seth's lies and I needed him to think we thought he was right," Jay explains, wincing.

"What did Blake say then?"

"Second star on the right and straight on." Jay shrugs. "It was jumbled. I thought at first he was already drugged at this time and wasn't in his right mind. Until we looked more at timing. I think he was just rushed. The call to you was after the drugs were in his system."

"When he knew he was dying," I finish. Taking a deep breath, I let the thoughts swirl inside. "He was giving you a clue to where the evidence is," I tell him. Jay's head snaps up, his eyes locking with mine.

"Second star on the right and straight on is a location," I explain.

Jay's eyes glaze over and he frowns in concentration. "Like a map?"

I laugh. "No, my brother was not that creative. I'm surprised he even remembered the line from the movie. It's Peter Pan."

Jay stares back at me at a total loss. "You've never seen it?" He shakes his head, I sigh.

"It's the way to Neverland," I tell him. Jay looks frustratingly at me. I can see when the understanding crashes into him. "The treehouse," he mutters. "Is it even still there?"

I shrug. "I haven't been there in years," I tell him. "If anything, it's a pile of wood by the tree."

Jay whips out his cell phone. "It's me. Get evidence and patrol to the Ramirez ranch. I'll meet you there in twenty."

We quickly dart back out to Jay's truck and take off toward Sarge's home. I lead Jay and the squad cars to the edge where the treehouse used to stand. After years of being abandoned, it's now overgrown with ivy. The bottom had caved out and the top smashed by a fallen branch. We wait while they search the area. My pulse zings with adrenaline that after all this time it had been hiding here.

"Found something!" a voice yells from inside the structure. The female officer slides back down the trunk, a black duffle bag in her hands. It's placed on the ground where it's photographed before opened and the contents taken out. Three plastic bags are placed next to the duffle. From where we're standing, it appears to be flash drives in one, picture prints in another, and a cell phone.

"No fucking way," Jay breathes out in relief next to me.

"That's what you were looking for?" I nod toward the scene.

"You have no idea." Jay shakes his head, a grin pulling at his lips. "This is going to change everything."

My heart races in excitement. "Way to go, bro," I whisper into the air, my eyes roaming over the remains of the treehouse. Part of me wonders if he knew Jay would find me and I'd figure out his message. Another part wonders if he knew he wouldn't make it out alive that night. A small slice of my heart feels comforted knowing he came here in his last few hours. A place that once brought joy. When times were innocent.

"They'll take it back to the lab and go over it. Our IT department will have to pick apart every frame and detail on those devices," Jay mutters.

"That sounds time consuming," I respond.

Jay's fingers scratch at the sides of his scalp. "Would have been better to have this five months ago. I can't believe I didn't figure it out sooner."

"You didn't know about the treehouse," I remind him, hoping to help ease the burden he feels.

Jay nods, turning to look at me thoughtfully. "Let's head home."

I smile, looping my arm through his. Jay brings me back to the truck and we ease away from the scene that is now roped off. He laces his fingers with mine on our drive back, cranking up the stereo as we go. After one song turns into another, I start to recognize the lineup, "The World I Know," Collective Soul.

Jay grins, gripping my hand tighter. "Blake made me one too." He hits the eject button. The silver disc slides out. My brother's handwriting scrawled *To McJ* over the front. I laugh. "He had the best taste in music," Jay says, pushing the CD back in to play.

I lean my head back, letting the lyrics settle into my heart, and I breathe in the night air. Ed Roland's vocals create chills down my arms. I squeeze Jay's hand, my feelings brimming over. A new normal is about to start. The world I previously knew has changed for the better. I'll forever miss my brother and I'm forever thankful for the life he gave me. We'll meet again someday. I'll make him proud and honor the sacrifice he made. My brother, my friend, my protector. Tenderly, I remember the past.

"He was the best," I agree with Jay.

The End

Epilogue

Four years later

"Well, I finally did it. Just like you imagined. I hope you know none of this would have been possible if it weren't for you," I tell the whitewashed headstone at my brother's grave. The sting of tears is fresh behind my eyeballs. I let my fingers run over the black lettering of his name. "I can't believe it's almost been five years," I murmur to myself.

Nearly five years have passed since the most devastating day of my young adult life. Now at almost twenty-three, I've lived my life the second chance it is, and it's all thanks to the two most important men in my life. My eyes flash over the grey rock and find Jay's while he waits for me, leaning against his new car. Suit coat and tie flapping in the breeze. The man can pull off a suit and I've been lucky enough the past few years to appreciate him in all his glory.

Jay stayed in Las Vegas while I worked on completing my

degree in the social services field. After everything Blake, the guys, and I went through, I knew I needed to do something to help other children and families like ours. My dream is to fix the foster care system and give children a better fighting chance. Jay is my biggest support and was behind me every step of the way. I lived on campus for one semester before he moved my stuff into his new home off-campus. It worked out perfect for us and any time he was away on a case usually coincided during my finals. I chalked this up to my brother watching over us.

"I'm scared to leave," I add, glancing back down at the headstone. "I love him and I'm scared to leave, but I know if I don't take this chance I'll never feel that I did enough for these families."

A month before graduation, I was offered a job through the same company I had completed my internship in. They were opening another branch, the only kicker was that it would require moving to Pennsylvania. I jumped at the chance to take it.

"He barely batted an eye," I confide in my brother. "He just told me to follow my dream. It's every girl's dream, only now I'm wondering if I was too hasty making this decision." A single tear falls now and I brush it away quickly. My black robe blows in the breeze around me, spinning the silver thread of the tassel in my hand. "I know you're not really here, that you're off somewhere in peace… I just… I wanted to say goodbye for now. I'll come back to visit, I promise. I love you and thank you so much." More tears slip out, my hands dive to my cheeks to wipe them away as I back away from Blake's resting spot.

No one ever said moving on would be easy. As time goes by, the gaping wound in my chest has shrunk and been repaired with a different kind of love. Knowing today was going to be my last day in Nevada was crushing. Good and bad memories bent with new and old and twisted around inside my heart. I find Jay's eyes again, his are soft as they watch me approach. He knew today was going to wreck me again even though it was also one of the happiest days of my life. In true Jay form, he was picking up from my lowest simply by loving me.

"You good?" he asks once I reach his side. His voice is gravelly and instantly gives my body the good kind of chills. His hand reaches for mine and he pulls me to him until I'm standing between his legs. I nod my head and lean forward until my forehead rests against his.

"This is harder than I thought it would be," I confess, my shoulders slumping. My body seeks Jay's and the comfort he gives.

"He'd understand, baby," Jay tells me before pulling back and using his fingers to lift my chin. "Blake wanted nothing but the best for you. And no one says this is permanent. If you want to change jobs in a few years and move back or move anywhere else, as long as it's for you, he wouldn't have minded."

I nod. "I know, it's still hard. I've never lived anywhere but here."

"You're going to be amazing," he tells me, placing a soft kiss on my lips.

My body sagging back into Jay. The words I've been holding onto for a month now are bursting to get out. I'm scared to see his reaction though. "I don't want to leave you," I tell him my biggest confession.

Jay's body turns to stone and for a second, I'm paralyzed with fear that he'll be mad or upset with me. I didn't give him a chance to really weigh in on my decision to leave. I more or less told him what I wanted to do and asked for his blessing. Jay's been unusually quiet about it. He's been more intense with my body like he's saying goodbye. I just assumed we'd make long-distance work for a few years, but we hadn't had *the* conversation about it.

"Do you mean that?" he asks, peering down at me. His eyes are intense, mixed with love, fear, and determination. I'm speechless, only managing to nod my head again.

"Why didn't you say anything?" he questions, moving our bodies so we're standing. His gaze slants down.

"I was scared," I admit, feeling ten shades of foolish at the same time. "I really want this job, Jay. I also want you. I don't know how to ask for both."

He exhales loudly, his whole body loosening on a giant sigh. "I was waiting to do this after your graduation ceremony today, but..." Jay reached into his front coat pocket, my heart stops and stammers before restarting. He pulls out a folded paper and hands it to me.

"What is it?" I ask, taking it from his fingers. I turn it over and read the words. My eyes snap to Jay's face, looking for any signs of a joke.

"It's a one-way ticket," he clarifies, his gaze holding mine. I feel warm everywhere, a happiness starting in my toes and blossoming within my chest.

"You're coming with me?" I gasp, throwing my arms around his neck.

"I put in my transfer request a while ago." He nods. "Lucky for me, a member of the Philadelphia team was retiring and they were willing to take me as a transfer."

"Oh my god," I breathe against his neck. "This is legit? We're going."

Jay nods, his arms holding me tighter. "I love you. I couldn't not try."

"Why didn't you say anything?" I ask.

"We didn't really talk about it." He loosens his grip and pulls back. "I wasn't sure you wanted me to follow you."

My throat clogs with emotion while my smile continues to get bigger. "I want to be anywhere you are," I tell him. "This is perfect."

"We should probably get going then," Jay announces, looking once more at the watch on his wrist. He helps me back into the car and we pull away. My eyes stay on the cemetery for as long as I can see it. Jay squeezes my hand reassuringly. I realize that I feel lighter and I'm actually looking forward to graduating and getting on the plane this evening. We got this. Jay's phone rings through the car, and he stills when he sees the name pop up.

"You're talking again?" I ask, tilting my chin. *T. Nich* flashes again.

"He's coming around." Jay shrugs, a hint of a smile plays on his lips.

"Well, he's only ignored you for two years," I answer, smiling. Men are sometimes just as bad as women with their drama. "You better answer."

Jay sighs, his finger hovering over the green answer button. "Before you overreact—"

Jay's cut off by Trent's swearing and yelling. I raise my eyebrows, laughing quietly. It's going to be a long drive.

More from A.M. Brooks

Scar (Trent's Story)- Winter 2020
Flesh – Summer 2020

www.ambrooksbooks.com
www.facebook.com/ambrooksbooks/
Twitter: @brooksauthor
Instagram: ambrooksbooks
Pinterest: www.pinterest.com/ambrooksbooks/

Made in the USA
Monee, IL
16 June 2020

32446986R00128